THE GLAD SUMMER

The Works of Jeffery Farnol:

THE BROAD HIGHWAY
THE MONEY MOON
THE AMATEUR GENTLEMAN
CHRONICLES OF THE IMP
THE HONOURABLE MR. TAWNISH
BELTANE THE SMITH
THE DEFINITE OBJECT
THE GESTE OF DUKE JOCELYN
OUR ADMIRABLE BETTY
BLACK BARTLEMY'S TREASURE
MARTIN CONISBY'S VENGEANCE
PEREGRINE'S PROGRESS
SIR JOHN DERING
THE LORING MYSTERY
THE HIGH ADVENTURE
THE QUEST OF YOUTH
GYFFORD OF WEARE
THE SHADOW
EPICS OF THE FANCY
ANOTHER DAY
OVER THE HILLS
THE JADE OF DESTINY
CHARMIAN, LADY VIBART
THE WAY BEYOND
WINDS OF FORTUNE
JOHN O' THE GREEN
A PAGEANT OF VICTORY
THE CROOKED FURROW
A BOOK FOR JANE
THE LONELY ROAD
THE HAPPY HARVEST
A NEW BOOK FOR JANE
A MATTER OF BUSINESS
ADAM PENFEATHER, BUCCANEER
MURDER BY NAIL
THE KING LIVETH
THE "PIPING TIMES"
HERITAGE PERILOUS
MY LORD OF WRYBOURNE
THE FOOL BELOVED
THE NINTH EARL

THE GLAD SUMMER

Being a truly Sentimental Idyll

BY

JEFFERY FARNOL

LONDON

SAMPSON LOW, MARSTON & CO., LTD.

First published 1951

MADE AND PRINTED IN GREAT BRITAIN BY PURNELL AND SONS, LTD.
PAULTON (SOMERSET) AND LONDON

Dedicated To
My daughter, CHARMIAN JANE
the devoted typist
and
Sternest Critic
of
her humble, highly respectful
sire:
JEFFERY FARNOL.

CONTENTS

CHAPTER   PAGE

I   TELLS OF THEIR FIRST, AND VERY UNPROPITIOUS, MEETING   I

II   TELLS HOW HARBOURNE CAME TO HARBOURNE .   7

III   TELLS WHY A CERTAIN LETTER WAS WRITTEN . .   15

IV   WHICH CONCERNS THIS SAME LETTER . . .   21

V   BEING MERELY A CHAPTER OF BUSINESS . . .   24

VI   HOW SIR NICHOLAS BECAME A HANDYMAN AND MET A SMALL THOUGH IMPORTANT PERSONAGE . .   29

VII   CONCERNING HOBNAILED BOOTS AND THE MAGIC OF CARDS   46

VIII   HOW NICHOLAS GLIMPSED THE SHADOW AGAIN— WITH THE REASON THEREFOR . . .   52

IX   OF BRUTALITY AND A BULL   57

X   CHIEFLY CONCERNING A BUTLER OF PRICE, THOUGH PRICELESS   63

XI   HOW (ACCORDING TO JOANNE) NOT TO MAKE LOVE .   71

XII   DIAMOND *v*. PASTE   77

XIII   HOW LORD WOLVERTON WROTE A LETTER, AND WHY   95

XIV   HOW A LETTER WAS BURNT AND PRISCILLA'S WOE TURNED TO JOY   103

XV   IN WHICH AUNT JEMIMA WONDERS   110

XVI   IN WHICH PRISCILLA POURS OUT TEA . . .   117

XVII   GIVES SOME DESCRIPTION OF A KISS . . .   127

XVIII   TELLS HOW NICHOLAS MET AN OLD SHIPMATE .   133

viii CONTENTS

CHAPTER		PAGE
XIX	IN WHICH NICHOLAS, BUILDING PIGSTIES, VERSIFIES	137
XX	CONCERNING THE BEAUTIES IN HAYMAKING . .	145
XXI	HOW THE "SPLENDORIOUS" IDEA INSPIRED ACTION	157
XXII	THE WHEREFORE OF BILL'S BLACK EYE . . .	165
XXIII	HARVEST	175
XXIV	DESCRIBES A HATE-FILLED LETTER	181
XXV	TELLS HOW SHE ASKED QUESTIONS AND HE TRIED TO ANSWER	185
XXVI	DESCRIBES A "SPLENDORIOUS" TEA-PARTY AND THE COMFORTING WISDOM OF AN AUNT . . .	191
XXVII	HOW AUNT JEMIMA ROSE TO THE OCCASION . .	200
XXVIII	WHICH, THOUGH THE LAST CHAPTER, IS NOT QUITE SO SENTIMENTAL AS MIGHT BE EXPECTED . .	207

CHAPTER I

*Tells of Their First, and Very Unpropitious,
Meeting*

IN THOSE now loftily disparaged "early Victorian days",
when England stood in the forefront of the nations, her
prestige so high and assured that none dared challenge it,
and her folk so simple-hearted as actually to believe in the
efficacy of prayer; in those happier, less tumultuous times
when the roads of England—though dusty in dry weather
and miry in wet—knew no greater peril than horse-drawn
vehicle, that is to say, before Death in the shape of petrol-
driven monsters had usurped the peaceful highways—on
such a day one, Nicholas Harbourne, was trudging wearily
southward.

The day was hot, the road dusty (of course), and himself direly athirst; thus with blissful visions of tankards
abrim with cool nutty ale, his eyes, beneath brows hoary
with dust, were keenly alert for sight of some alehouse
or hedge-tavern where he might find this so needed re-
freshment. Thus presently, at a place where three roads
met, he beheld a dusty fingerpost that announced in faded
lettering: "To Tetbury. To Bowey St. Mary. To Harbourne". Here he paused, but, seeing no sign of any inn
and thus having no choice of direction, he sat down, with

dusty back against dusty fingerpost, to wait for some way-farer to direct him.

And after some while, borne to him on the warm, som-nolent air, came a sound of slow-plodding hoofs with the creak and rumble of heavy wheels, and, glancing thither-wards, he beheld, drawn by two powerful horses very shaggy as to manes and fetlocks, a great wain or farm-wagon painted sky-blue and mounted on the pinkest wheels he had ever seen. Nicholas sat up to blink at this garish vehicle and hail the driver:

"Ahoy, Bill! Bring to and tell me, like the honest Bill you are, where is the nearest inn, tavern or alehouse? Speak, Bill, speak!"

The driver reined up his team with a jerk to stare down as his questioner round-eyed, took off his old straw hat to scratch his shock of towlike hair and, thus scratching and staring, exclaimed:

"Love me precious innards! 'Ow du ee know as I be Bill, for Bill I be sure-ly—and, this so being, 'ow should ee know as sich be so?"

"Because Bill is writ large all over you, so Bill the word is—ale! Lead me to it and let us drink to the Bill that you are and the me that I am. What say you, Bill?"

"Sir, I says ar, very fervent and 'earty. So ef ee'll mount up along o' me I'll drive ee to Joe Todgers' Peck o' Malt."

With a certain (seaman's) lithe nimbleness Nicholas swung up to driving-seat, Bill chirruped to his horses, and on rumbled the four great pink wheels; remembering which, Nicholas remarked:

"Your master certainly likes bright colours."

"Sir, my master ain't a him, she's a her, being a lady. Mistus Joanne Marsden as farms Fallowdene like her folks afore her, and she had me and Jarge paint this here old wagin bright-like, 'oping mebbe 'twould so fetch a extry pound or so at the sale."

"What sale, Bill?"

"Why, her sale, sir. She've got to sell up and go along o' this yere noo landlord, Sir Nicholas, 'aving rose the rents and ruinated her—ar and others, too, dang 'im! So Mistus Joanne has gotter go."

"Where to, Bill?"

"Well, she've got a bit of a cottage wi' three or four acres as was left to her by her dear mother."

"When is the sale?"

"In about six weeks, sir, and a sad day 'twill be for arl on us at Fallerdene—sure-ly!"

"Your mistress is a middle-aged lady, rather bony and with grey hair, eh, Bill?"

"Well, 'ardly that, sir, seein' as 'ow she be just turned twenty-five and 'er 'air being red—leastways sometimes, when the sun ketches it right. And as for bones——"

"Well, what about 'em, Bill?"

"Sir, there be so much soft white prettiness about 'em as you wouldn' know she 'ad a bone about 'er."

"And, being a farmer, hayrakes, pitchforks, and so on, I suppose she's fairly hard and muscular?"

"Ay, 'er can toss a sheaf wi' the best."

"And in wet weather up to her eyes in mud, Bill?"

"Ay, 'er don't mind a bit o' mud—nor dung neither —and yon's the Peck o' Malt."

Before this small, sequestered alehouse Bill reined up, roaring as he did so:

"Oho, Joe—house! Oho! Ale, Joe, ale! Wheer be ee, I wonder."

"Why, here for sure," and out from the lattice a face scowled up at them.

"Well, two pints, Joe."

"Three," said Nicholas, "for you'll pray join us." The scowl vanished, the head nodded, vanished also; and when they entered the small cool taproom they found Joe with three foaming tankards awaiting them. So, having nodded and pledged each other, these three tankards were slowly elevated, emptied, and sighed over blissfully.

Nicholas ordered their replenishment. Thus presently again the three heads nodded, the tankards were raised —then suddenly arrested, as from the road came sound of trampling horse-hoofs and therewith a voice, richly sweet but commanding, cried:

"Bill, come you here!"

"My mistus!" He gasped and, gulping the last of his ale, stepped out, followed by Nicholas, who beheld a feminine shapeliness in riding habit (dusty, of course); a young woman this, whose brows were too black, whose ruddy, full-lipped mouth was too wide, and whose chin, just now set aggressively, was quite too masculine.

Raising dusty hat, Nicholas bowed, saying:

"Madam, the fault is entirely mine——"

"Oh!" she exclaimed, frowning more angrily. "And pray who may you be?"

"I," said Nicholas, moved by sudden impulse, "am your very humble servant—Anthony Anson."

"And, Mistus, 'e were choked wi' dust and fair perishing o' thirst——"

"Indeed, he looks very unpleasantly dusty, Bill."

"Miss Marsden, I am so compact of and disguised in dust that, when less so, I shall venture to present myself for your better appraisal, for, devoid of dust, I show so much better than at present. I shall hope to afford you a pleasant surprise."

"Sir, your overwhelming self-confidence indeed surprises me, and——"

"Miss Marsden, I am a surprising person and shall hope to amaze, astound and astonish you sometime when we are better acquainted."

"Mr. Anson, I have no least desire for your acquaintance."

"Miss Marsden, I am bold to think such desire will grow upon you until it becomes an obsession."

"What nonsense!" She laughed. "Or should I frown at your presumption?"

"Either," he answered gravely. "I venture to prophesy the end will be the same."

"What end, pray?"

"The future—and we can neither of us evade our destiny."

"Mr. Anson, you become mysterious and I detest riddles, so I will leave you to guzzle your ale. You, Bill, get going before this—this talkative gentleman makes you quite drunk." So saying, she gave her horse its head and cantered away through the sunshine.

"Yes," said Nicholas, watching the lithe grace of her as she rode, "you were right, Bill."

"'Ow so, sir?"

"About her hair—it is coppery when the sun catches it right."

CHAPTER II

Tells How Harbourne Came to Harbourne

AT HARBOURNE Nicholas took leave of Bill and, as the sky-blue wagon rumbled away, stood to look about him upon this most beautiful of villages, with its grey old church, its cosy inn and thatched cottages, their gardens abloom with flowers—all clustered about a pleasant green, shaded by trees, most especially one, seemingly old, well nigh on the church, its mighty branches wide spread. But just at present the usual peaceful hush of this sleepy hamlet was broken by the clamour of troublous voices where labourers, returning from field and farmstead, stood to talk while their womenfolk, in garden and open cottage doorways, looked and listened, shrilling an angry question every now and then; and oftenest recurring, uttered by voices woefully distressed or voices that growled in futile anger, were the three words: "Sir Nicholas Harbourne."

Now on a seat built around the massive trunk of the aforementioned great old tree on the green two smock-frocked ancients sat cheek by jowl discussing the iniquity of landlords in general and their own new landlord in particular, on this wise:

"I tell ee, Job, 'e should be took and 'ung, ar and jibbeted likewise!"

"No, shot, 'Enery; shot, neat and soldierly."

"Shootin' be too good for the likes o' 'e, Job!"

"Ay, mebbe so. 'Owsever, I'd like to get at 'im wi' my old baggonet—in 'is bowels——"

"No, I tell ee as 'e should be took and 'ung——"

"Meaning your new landlord, of course," said Nicholas, pausing beside them.

"Ay," nodded old Henry fiercely, " 'im as be our curse and ruination."

"Ar!" growled old Job, " 'im as be tekking the clothes off'n our backs and the bread from our children, dang 'im. And 'ow says you, young master?"

"That any landlord who would so misuse his people would deserve hanging."

"Or get my old baggonet in 'is bowels, eh, sir?" demanded old Henry.

"Well, yes, even that."

"Young man, though ee be so young, you got uncommon good sense—eh, Job?"

"Ar, no question, 'Enery."

"Why, then," said Nicholas, "my good sense suggests three pints at the inn yonder; how say you, Job and Henry?"

As one man the ancients arose and, as one, they replied:

"Ar, drackly minute, sir."

"With j'y, and thankee, sir."

So, walking between these two hearty old fellows, Nicholas crossed the wide green and with them entered a certain snug room in this cosy inn of The Soaring Lark. Here they were greeted by a cheery man, very trim as to person, who beamed at them from between a pair of prodigious fiery whiskers, nodded to the ancients, but pulled a non-existent forelock at Nicholas and "made a leg" as only a man-o'-warsman could; wherefore, smiling also, Nicholas enquired:

"How long since you swallowed the anchor, messmate?"

"E'cod, sir," exclaimed the landlord, beaming more than ever, "you've a sailorly eye, for sure! I quit the Navy just afore they spi'led it with steam, being bosun's mate aboard the old *Canopus,* eighty-four. Ah, them was the days, sir!" So saying, he vanished, to return with a tray whereon stood three tankards topped by creamy foam. Together the ancients grasped a tankard and together they spoke:

"Good 'ealth, sir!"

"Long life to ee, maister!"

Then together they puffed away the foam, sipped, quaffed deep, and sighed, while Nicholas, beckoning the landlord, enquired:

"Pray, bosun, what's your name?"

"Will Lawler, sir, at your service."

"I am Anthony Anson, a stranger hereabouts, and I'm wondering if you could find room—quarters for me here."

"Quarters, sir?" repeated the bosun, grappling his larboard whisker. "Meaning board an' lodging, and for how long?"

"Oh, say a month or so."

"Why, as to that, sir," said Bosun Will, giving a tug at his whisker, "I'll have to consult the commander; ex-cuse me!" And away he strode, leaving Nicholas to chat with the ancients and listen to the harsh rumble of angry voices from the adjacent tap-room. And after some while back came the bosun, followed by his "commander", a gentle-eyed woman so comely of face and form that instinctively Nicholas smiled and rose as the bosun said:

"Sir, here is my wife—and commander! Kitty m' lass, this be the gentleman, Mr. Anson, as wishes to bide with us a spell."

"Oh, but, sir," she murmured shyly, "us be nowise used to lodgers, specially o' the quality; us do be very simple folk, sir."

"Good!" exclaimed Nicholas heartily. "For, Mrs. Law-ler, I am such a very simple fellow that I like all simple things, four walls, a roof and a donkey's breakfast——"

"He means a straw mattress!" chuckled the bosun.

"'Deed, sir," she smiled, "us can do better nor that. There be a spare room above stairs and a true goose-feather bed! Go wi' me, sir, if you please, and I'll show ee." She led him up a somewhat narrow stair and across a wide landing into a chamber redolent of lavender and so much more than he expected that for the moment he was dumb—mistaking which silence, Mrs. Lawler sighed:

"The carpet's sadly worn in places, sir, the ewer be cracked and the wash-basin chipped, likewise the arm-chair bean't so good as it looks, but 'tis a real feather bed, sir. Yet if this'll soot ee——"

"Admirably!" he exclaimed fervently. "Mrs. Lawler, I feel at home already!"

"Then as to your meals, sir? I be only the plainest o' plain cooks——"

"Indeed no!" he retorted. "There is nothing plain about you!" At this she flushed and dimpled, saying:

"Well, Mr. Anson, if you can put up wi' we, us can put with ee, sure-ly!"

"Mrs. Lawler, I am extremely grateful! Now as to your terms per week?"

"Well, sir," she answered nervously, "if you think a pound a week right——"

"I do not—we'll make it two."

"Oh, but, sir——"

"Mrs. Lawler, considering that feather bed, we ought to make it more."

"Oh no, sir, no! Two pound be too much."

"And here is a fortnight's rent in advance."

"Four pound!" she murmured. "I don't know what my Will'll say. I'll go an' ax him." So away she sped, leaving Nicholas to survey the homely comfort about him with ever-growing content. And after some while to him came Bosun Will, who, having smoothed each fiery, tameless whisker, touched his eyebrow and said:

"Sir, my commander and self, having took counsel con-sarning your too generous offer, begs leave to split the difference, making it one pound ten and very generous indeed."

"As you will, Will, old seadog; here's my hand on it with my undying respect for the Navy and especially Bosun Will."

"Honoured, sir!" growled the bosun as they shook hands.

"Well now," said Nicholas, "I've a couple of valises in Horsham at the King's Head; how about them, Will?"

"Sir, my man Ned shall fetch 'em in the gig at once."

"Thanks, Will. And now I suggest ale; how say you?"

"Thankee, sir, but ale being ale, me me, and my commander the commander, I don't drink except when by thirst com-pelled thereto; wherefore, sir, I begs you'll ex-cuse me not therein bearing you company."

Now before this cosy inn pleasantly shaded by trees stood a spacious oaken settle, and here, seated in the sunset glow, tankard on knee, Nicholas gazed wistfully about him on this beautiful village, where this evening, instead of drowsy peace and rustic content, haggard-eyed trouble stirred, while from the taproom nearby voices, louder now and fiercer than ever, uttered fearsome threats and curses against Sir Nicholas Harbourne. Roused presently by sound of approaching horse-hoofs, and glancing round, Nicholas beheld Mistress Joanne Marsden riding slowly towards him, therefore he rose to salute her, hat in one hand, ale-pot in the other, saying:

"Good evening, marm!"

"No—no it is not!" she retorted, checking her horse the better to say it. "This is a bad—a cruel, wicked evening and must be only the first of others—to bring misery upon us every one and ruin to many! And all this the doing of one hatefully, wickedly selfish wretch, a brute I will not foul my lips to name!"

"Then, of course," said Nicholas, "you can only mean Sir Nicholas Harbourne."

"Yes, I do! But what can you, a stranger, know about the wretch?"

"That nobody seems to love him——"

"Love him?" she cried and quite ferociously. "I should think not indeed! Who would or could love such a hateful, heartless tyrant? He is a two-legged abomination, a walking pestilence, an all-pervading blight!"

"A most exact description," said Nicholas, "and, as such, he should be done away with. But how? I have heard it suggested he should be hanged, shot or stabbed, and lately, from the taproom yonder, further suggestions that he should be drowned, strangled, burnt at the stake, and cut to pieces with scythes. Pray, marm, which method do you favour?"

"All of them!" she answered, with fierce nod.

"Which, of course, means none of them."

"Oh, I suppose so!" she sighed. "But, anyhow, he is a brute beast."

"No," said Nicholas gravely, but with dark eyes twinkling, "let him remain your Two-legged Abomination. Yes, indeed, 'tis a phrase to cherish in one's memory! And now, marm, if you happen to need a handyman, I have one to offer you, a worthy fellow, marm——"

"Do—not call me 'marm'—as if I were an old woman!"

"An extremely worthy fellow, madam, in every respect, respectful and highly respectable——"

"Meaning yourself, I suppose?"

"Precisely, madam!"

"Well, what can this so worthy fellow do?"

"Anything in reason, Mistress Joanne."

"Now, sir, you become familiar!"

"But most respectfully and in all humility, dear my lady——"

"Now you are as odiously fulsome!"

"Yet with meekest sincerity. But as regards your would-be handyman——"

"Well," she demanded, "can this so worthy fellow milk a cow?"

"I fear the art is beyond him—for the present."

"Can he plough a straight furrow?"

"Straight as an arrow—with practice."

"Can he thatch a rick, use a scythe, swing a flail or lay a hedge?"

"These are accomplishments he has yet to attain. But with hammer, saw, plane, adze and chisel, you will find him perfectly competent, indeed admirably proficient. Then, besides, he is clean, honest, willing, industrious and remarkably abstemious——"

"So I remark!" she retorted, gesturing towards the tankard in his hand; then she laughed, shook her handsome head and rode away at a graceful canter.

Now, glancing somewhat ruefully at his tankard, Nicholas emptied it at a gulp and, sitting down again, agreed with himself that Joanne was a quaint and lovely name; that, being more than pretty, she must be handsome; that, although grimly valiant of soul, she was also intensely feminine and thus might and could be sweetly gentle and therefore—perfectly adorable. Having arrived at this conclusion, he sighed, rose and, stepping indoors, was there welcomed by Mrs. Lawler with smiling curtsy and the words:

"Sir, your supper be ready—though 'tis only a small duckling, stuffed, and wi' fresh-picked green peas—but cooked very plain——"

"Hurrah!" he exclaimed in muted rapture. "Mrs. Lawler, pray take my grateful hand, ma'm, and lead me to it."

CHAPTER III

Tells Why a Certain Letter was Written

FOR A week Nicholas rambled to and fro about this vast Harbourne estate, visiting every sequestered hamlet and village, and everywhere found misery—saw and heard so much of futile anger, haggard anxiety for the future and distress for the present, that he was deeply stirred, more especially upon two occasions, first as thus:

Upon a sunny afternoon he was exploring a certain leafy, winding by-lane, when he heard what he believed to be the doleful mewing of a cat, until, turning a sudden corner, he beheld an aged woman crouched upon grassy bank, white head bowed between clutching hands, and knew this odd sound for the voice of her strangled weeping; so he approached and, guessing her answer, enquired, gently:

"Grandmother, what is your trouble?"

"Go—way!" she snarled, with feeble though furious gesture. "I don't want nobody, so lemme be!"

Seating himself beside this desolate old creature, he set his arm about her and repeated his question:

"Granny, pray what is your trouble?"

Now his arm was so strong and comforting, his voice so gently compelling, that, despite her gasping sobs, she told him:

"The cottage yonder . . . tidn't very big . . . but it held all my earthly happiness. . . . 'Twas there my Tom brought me . . . his bride. 'Twas there my three boys was born . . . 'twas there my deary Tom died! And now, in a little while, I . . . must leave it."

"Why, Granny?"

"B' reason as they rose the rent again, and 'tis beyond my strength to earn. . . . I be too old to work like as I could and did."

"Then what shall you do now?"

"Creep away to hide myself and die and . . . the sooner the better."

"Lord no, Grandma, that will never do. . . ."

"Well, then, what can I do?" she demanded fiercely. "Tell me that, will ee!"

"Why, to be sure," he replied, somewhat at a loss. "There is always the future and hope for better times."

"'Ope?" she repeated bitterly. "'Ope died long ago, and the best never no wise come my way since my deary Tom took and died."

"Well," said Nicholas, more at a loss than ever, "do you—believe in prayer?"

"I did, but I don't and never shall no more, not me—no! I prayed the Lord to bring my three sojer sons safe back t' me—but He let 'em all be killed and buried far away . . . overseas! I prayed the Lord to spare my Tom, but, even while I prayed . . . my dear Tom died! So I'm never a-goin' to pray no more, not me—no!"

"How long is it before you must leave your cottage, Granny?"

"Only fifteen days!" she sighed, struggling to her feet with his ready aid.

"And, pray, Granny, what is your name?"

"I be Mrs. Mills, old Becky Mills as nobody don't love and as don't love nobody neither—not me!" And up she reared her old, white head defiantly. "Ah, well, young man, you've talked me out o' my fullish tears and for that I thank ee—ay, and I hope the Lord God'll treat ee kinder than He've used me!" So saying, she hobbled across the lane and into her little cottage, slamming the stout door against him—and the cruel world in general.

The second occasion was at evening time as he stood where he might look down upon that farmstead called Fallowdene.

A stately old house ruddy of brick, creamy of plaster, its massive timbers richly carved, like the heavy bargeboards of its steep gables, a gracious old house mellowed by time and loving care to a thing of beauty. Behind the house was a spacious rickyard with thatched barns and stabling, beyond which lay yellow cornfields and lush meadows, while before and beside this ancient house were smooth lawns edged with blooming flowerbeds, and a paddock where two sleek horses cropped the grass, and before this again a walled kitchen-garden and shady orchard. Distant figures he saw busied at their divers labour, but nowhere any sight of the one form his keen gaze was seeking.

Descending the hill, Nicholas approached until he reached the orchard wall, to pause there instinctively.

And thus he became aware of yet another woman's grief, but this time nowise hushed or strangled, for this woman sobbed and wept unrestrainedly. Reaching up long arms, Nicholas drew himself up with the utmost caution until he could peep over the wall, and thus beheld her lying face down beneath an apple tree nearby, outstretched in the very abandonment of grief.

With the same extremity of caution Nicholas lowered himself to stand in no little perplexity, pondering what was best to do about it and in what possible manner to check this all too passionate grief; thus he deliberated, until, moved by sudden inspiration, he took off his hat and tossed it over the wall, aiming for that particular tree beneath which she lay. . . . The weeping stopped instantly; Nicholas began whistling an old sea shanty and, having given the weeper time to dry her eyes and compose herself, drew himself up and was astride the wall in as many moments.

"Oh—you!" she exclaimed, whereat Nicholas turned, made pretence to start violently, checked his whistling and answered:

"Myself, marm!"

"Of course!" said she angrily, rising the better to frown up at him. "It could be—only you!"

"Yes, merely me myself, marm."

"Why did you throw your nasty old hat at me?"

"Not at you, marm, only towards you."

"What for? And do—not—call me 'marm'."

"That I might follow it, Miss Joanne—like this!" And, speaking, down he leapt within a yard of her.

"I think you are a most outrageously audacious wretch!"

"And yet," he sighed, looking as meek as possible, "my audacity is tempered with a very real humility."

"Why are you trespassing here?"

"First for my hat and——"

"Oh, take it and go!"

"I will. But first may this most humble wretch venture again to ask if he can help you—I mean can you find him work of any kind?"

"No—ah, no!" she replied, with sound very like a sob. "You are too late! I am giving up the farm. . . . Aunt Jemima, little Priscilla and I must leave, and we . . . are going dreadfully soon!"

"Who says so, pray?"

"I say so!"

"But you are merely a very young, extremely human woman, and, being so, are probably mistaken."

"Oh, if I only were! But I'm not."

"Are you so sure?"

"Of course I'm sure, too hatefully sure and perfectly certain."

"But is anything certain in this world, and can anyone be sure of the future?"

"Yes—I am, because I know."

"But my dear child——"

"I'm neither yours nor a child!"

"However, no mere human, young or old, man or woman, can possibly know what is not yet and yet therefore to be."

"That sounds absolute nonsense!"

"Yet in it is more sense, Miss Joanne, than you sense, despite your sense, common or otherwise, seems able to sense."

"Meaning I am not only a 'mere woman' but a fool

beside. Well now, hateful trespasser, I think you had better go."

"This moment!" he agreed and, putting on his hat, swung himself up and back astride the wall. But here he paused to remove his hat again, saying very tenderly:

"Poor, dear, silly child, don't cry until you are really hurt, or cross bridges till they're really there, or trouble trouble till trouble troubles you; in a word—don't worry!"

"Oh," she murmured brokenly, "it isn't . . . trite phrases I need . . . but strength to . . . comfort me. . . ." Now as she spoke, these eyes that Nicholas was sure now were the gentlest, loveliest and most beautiful he had ever seen, brimmed with sudden tears as, turning swiftly to hide them, she sped away, weeping again and more bitterly than ever.

Wherefore and therefore Nicholas, seated this same evening in his cosy bed-sitting-room, wrote a letter, which, though brief, was to cause widespread commotion, alter the lives of many and, with them, his own.

CHAPTER IV

Which Concerns this Same Letter

MR. JOSIAH BIGGS, portly, imposing, and senior partner of Messrs. Biggs, Dyke and Biggs, attorneys at law, stared in shocked amazement at the letter he had just perused, flounced in his chair till it creaked in protest, rang the bell violently and shouted at the clerk who answered this summons:

"Send Mr. Arthur to me!"

And presently Mr. Arthur appeared, a placid, gentlemanly person in blond whiskers and the usual garments, on whom Mr. Biggs glared and at whom he shook the letter, exclaiming:

"Arthur, the young fool must be stark, staring mad!"

"Who, Father?"

"I say utterly bereft of his wits, demented, and ready for the madhouse! He should be clapped into Bedlam at once!"

"Why, Father?"

"Never, no—never in all my long experience of human folly have I ever known such an amazingly preposterous, not to say scandalously revolutionary and therefore utterly damnable, suggestion!"

"What, Father?"

"This wildly absurd, perfectly insane letter! Read it;

no—I will! Sit, Arthur; sit and listen!" Here Mr. Biggs, senior, flounced again, scowled, cleared his throat resoundingly and read:

" 'Gent'—pray remark the absurd abbreviations—'Gent: On June six, prox., all rents on my Harbourne estates are to be cut by half, viz. fifty p.c. Faithfully, Nicholas Harbourne.' And what d'you say to this, Arthur?"

"That I am pleasantly surprised, sir."

"Eh? What? Pleasantly?"

"Yes, Father. I liked Sir Nicholas at our first interview, and this enhances my esteem."

"Good . . . great . . . heavens above! But this proves him a madman, a revolutionary, a—a confounded radical who will ruin the country!"

"On the contrary, sir, I venture to say that by this beneficent act in thus relieving his tenantry he will help the country to greater prosperity."

"Arthur," cried his sire in horrified tone, "you perfectly astonish and confound me!"

"And, Father, permit me to retort that you astonish me no less."

"Ha, do I, sir, do I? How, pray?"

"By allowing this fellow Wolf, the bailiff, to so blind you to the welfare of the Harbourne tenantry, to so misdirect you that you have permitted him thus to raise the rents again, the second time in five years, which I pronounce to be sheer tyranny——"

"Oh, do you, sir, do you? It seems you also are influenced by these damnable radical ideas, hey? However, young Harbourne's preposterous folly shall be nipped in the bud, cut short, ended forthwith. . . . Well, what now?" he demanded as, with gentle rap, a clerk peeped in fearfully to announce:

"Sir Nicholas Harbourne, gentlemen?"

"Bid him wait until——"

"I'm here!" said Nicholas, and in he strode, light of step and blithe of look, as usual. He nodded gaily to sire, shook hands heartily with son, tossed hat and gloves into one chair, seated himself in another, and said cheerily:

"Now, Mr. Biggs, you may begin."

CHAPTER V

Being Merely a Chapter of Business

MR. BIGGS, senior, flounced and cleared his throat again, twiddled his thumbs, shook his head portentously and finally spoke.

"Sir Nicholas, your letter has deeply perturbed and greatly shocked me, need I say——"

"Oh no; I expected it would, and I'm here to shock you more, just a little."

"Merciful heavens!" exclaimed Mr. Biggs. "What more?"

"I desire to make over a small cottage known as Mills Cot, together with three or four acres, to its present tenant, Mrs. Rebecca Mills, this property to be hers to have and to hold in perpetuity. I rather like that phrase, so pray use it."

"A gift, Sir Nicholas?"

"Absolutely! Let the deed be drawn up or executed at once; I'll sign it before I go." Mr. Biggs rose from his chair, gulped, glowered and—sat down again.

"As regards my remission and lowering of all rents, you will deal with this at once; also I desire you will have this information printed on sheets in bold, clear lettering, easy to read, and a copy dispatched to each of my tenants, and this I repeat—at once."

Mr. Biggs seemed to find some difficulty with his breathing, also in choosing words adequate to the occasion; at last with gesture almost threatening, he spoke:

"Young man . . . sir, you will now listen to me and to reason——"

"Are these synonymous?" laughed Nicholas, whereat sire frowned and gulped again while son smiled and nodded gently. Sire therefore continued the more heatedly:

"Sir Nicholas, having been so recently a merchant seaman, you are therefore profoundly ignorant, especially of land values. I must now inform you that all property, more especially in the counties of Kent and Sussex, have lately much increased in value and will continue so to do."

"Mr. Biggs, I rejoice to hear it!"

"Consequently, sir, all rents have been and will be raised accordingly!"

"Mr. Biggs, I am grieved to hear it and refuse to allow it! Instead, as I have informed you very plainly, all my rents are coming down."

"Sir Nicholas, this must not be, since it is bad for you and worse for the county generally."

"But good for my tenants in particular. So, as I say, you will have these notices printed in good, bold type——"

"Sir, I beg you will listen to me!"

"No, Mr. Biggs; instead you shall listen to me! So pray lend me your ears, both of 'em! Before inheriting these vast estates, so very unexpectedly, from my unlovely uncle, Sir Jonas, I was earning, as first officer aboard the Indiaman *Etruria,* just sufficient for my comfort, and my quarters measured roughly twelve feet by ten! Today, as you told me at our last interview, my income is somewhere about twenty-five thousand pounds a year with land stretching from the Downs to the sea. Added to this, I own a town mansion and in the country a great barn of a house too big for comfort and impossible ever to make a home——"

"Sir," cried Mr. Biggs indignantly, "Sir Nicholas, I protest! Grayladies is one of the grandly noble mansions of Old England! A famous and historic monument, once a splendid abbey, or some such, until Bluff King Hal bestowed it upon your ancestor, Sir Richard Harbourne, for valour in the field. Ah, a grand and noble structure is Grayladies."

"Which," said Nicholas, "makes me wonder what became of the Gray Ladies, poor dears!"

"Sir, history does not record! But returning to the subject of our discussion: by your rash and reckless, ill-considered act you would reduce your present income by half——"

"Leaving myself over twelve thousand a year, which I consider fairly adequate to the needs of any ignorant merchant seaman, especially such very simple person as myself."

"But, Sir Nicholas, you are no longer a seaman, and I prove you anything but simple. Today, sir, you are a baronet of long and noble ancestry; today you are a power in the country, and your responsibilities therefore correspondingly many and great."

"Especially as regards my tenantry!"

"But most especially to yourself, sir. You now have a great, a lofty social position which must be lived up to! Your noble mansion in London with its retinue of servants, besides the magnificence of Grayladies, will be extremely costly to maintain."

"How many servants have I?"

"In your town house they number ten, sir; at Grayladies, within doors, male and female, they number thirty-five."

"Lord!" sighed Nicholas. "And all to look after me?"

"Besides these, sir, you employ fifteen gardeners, five gamekeepers, and nine grooms, and, of course, your bailiff, Mr. Wolf, and his two assistants."

"Making seventy-seven in all. Damme, I've worked an Indiaman with fewer hands!"

"So you perceive, Sir Nicholas, these will and must be a first charge on your income."

"Not so, Mr. Biggs—a dis-charge. You will rid me of all these unwanted servants at once and close both useless houses."

"Cl-close them?" stammered Mr. Biggs, aghast.

"Immediately!"

"But . . . good . . . great . . . heavens!" gasped Mr. Biggs. "The houses will go to rack and ruin! The magnificent park and gardens at Grayladies will become a wilderness!"

"Well, keep a brace of gardeners and put caretakers in the houses, or, better still, sell them."

"Sell them?" repeated Mr. Biggs in voice faint with horror.

"Whichever course you deem best," said Nicholas. "These are my orders! And pray don't forget those notices must be in boldest, clearest type. So, gentlemen, for the present, goodbye. Harbourne calls me, for, between you and me and the deed-boxes yonder, I'm after a farm-labourer's job, which, by hook or crook, I mean to secure." Then, taking hat and gloves, Nicholas bowed to speechless sire, shook hands with smiling son and strode blithely away.

"A—a farm labourer!" gasped Biggs, senior, so soon as he could speak. "He's mad, as I suspected! A stark, raving lunatic and should be shut up! Arthur, in heaven's name what—what are you smiling at?"

"A farm labourer, sir!"

CHAPTER VI

How Sir Nicholas Became a Handyman and Met a Small Though Important Personage

A WEEK had elapsed, and today every village on the Harbourne estate was in a ferment by reason of a certain notice printed in extremely bold type, easy to decipher, and which, being read, stirred all readers and hearers to deep and varying emotions, first of disbelief, changing to doubt, to awed wonder, to hope, and finally to rapturous joy. Women laughed, men cheered. While in a certain spacious kitchen, where Miss Jemima Marsden, with Ann, the first housemaid, was making and baking bread, with other goodly things, Joanne, dimpled elbows on table and head in hands, sat gazing down at another of these notices, staring at each bold-printed word beneath brows knit in troubled perplexity.

"No!" she repeated. "No, Aunt Jemima! I cannot, I will not, I—dare not believe it. Such wonders don't happen, and this is so—so unnatural and too good to be true!"

Busied with rolling-pin, Aunt Jemima, this ever serene, gentle-eyed lady, answered placidly:

"However, my dearest, should this marvel be true indeed, which I dare to believe, we shall not be compelled to leave this dear old house, this beloved home of ours."

"If it be true," repeated Joanne wistfully, "oh, if it really and truly is true, then Sir Nicholas Harbourne must be a—masculine angel!"

"He is certainly magnanimous, my dear, a very noble gentleman!"

"And old, of course, Aunt! He must be very, very old and kind! No young man could ever possibly be so unselfish."

In at the open lattice came Bill's towlike head to say in awed tones:

"Mistus Joanne, this yere be a merricle! To raise our rents be nat'ral, to lower 'em ain't! So me and Jarge and Joe, ar, and all on us, do reckon as 'tis a merricle, sure-ly, no question! You don't 'ave to sell up and leave this old place now, eh, Miss Jo?"

"Not now, Bill, thank God!"

"Ar! And Sir Nicholas 'Arbourne likewise! Lord love 'is old white head."

"Oh, then he is old, is he, Bill?"

"Ma'am, 'e must be! Only a old chap as be past wishin' for wine, women and song would give back s' much money to the good land and the likes o' we——"

"Good morning!" said a cheerful voice, and in beside Bill's shaggy poll came the sleek, dark head of Nicholas. "Bill has just been telling me the news."

"Ar, so I 'ave, mistur, 'bout this yere meracklous merricle."

"Which," said she, turning towards Nicholas, "I hardly dare believe even yet, because it seems too wonderful, too nobly generous for belief! But if it is true—oh, then he must be an old darling, a grandly noble old gentleman."

"Who, pray?"

"Why, Sir Nicholas Harbourne, of course! I should love to kiss his dear, wrinkled old face!"

"Should you indeed, Miss Joanne?"

"Yes, indeed I should, his dear old silvery head, yes and every wrinkle of his angel face—because if this is true, as I am beginning to believe, he is the grandest, kindest, most unselfish landlord that ever was or could be!"

"And so," said Nicholas, dwelling on the word, "you would like to—kiss—him?"

"Yes, repeatedly!"

"He would be glad to know it."

"Well, he never will, of course."

"You might perhaps write and tell him so."

"Goodness gracious, as if I'd dare! I haven't your cool audacity! Oh, Aunt Jemima, this is my trespasser who hurled his hat at me, as I told you. Mr. Anson, my aunt, Miss Marsden."

Aunt Jemima, viewing him with those gentle though keenly appraising eyes of hers, curtsied above and over her floury rolling-pin, saying:

"May all trespassers be as welcome!"

Nicholas bowed above and over the window-sill, answering and with grave sincerity:

"Miss Marsden, I am truly grateful——"

"So are we," sighed Joanne, "Aunt and I, to Sir Nicholas Harbourne, blessings on his grand old white head, because he has saved this dear old place to us. There will be no sale now."

"Good!" said Nicholas. "Then perhaps you can find

room about the place for the clean, respectable, highly intelligent handyman I proffer for your acceptance."

"Meaning Mr. Anson, Mr. Anson?"

"That same, madam."

"But would Mr. Anson mind Mr. Anson having to perform such rough work as I might ask Mr. Anson to do?"

"Miss Joanne, Mr. Anson, being Mr. Anson, would perform as only Mr. Anson could, can and would."

"Then if Mr. Anson will be content with the miserable pittance of ten shillings a week, all I dare offer at present, Mr. Anson may consider himself engaged as our man-of-all-work."

"To which offer, mistress, Mr. Anson replies: 'Done!' So now, pray what is your first order?"

"They pigsties!" said Bill. "Us can't nowise raise pigs till they'm repaired, and pigs pays right proper they do, mistus!"

"I know," she sighed, "but we can't afford pigs yet, Bill."

"No, 'm! 'Ows'ever, the old tithe barn wants its door mended, bad."

"It needs a new door, Bill, but we daren't afford that either."

"Mistress Joanne, your handyman shall do his best with what remains of the old one."

"Sir, that bit of old door be beyond repairin', purty nigh, no question."

"Yes," said Joanne, with another sigh, "I'm afraid it is; yes, even beyond the power of such handyman as Mr. Anson, Mr. Anson."

"Nevertheless, mistress mine, he shall have a go at it. Come, Bill, show me where."

"Ay, sir, but there bean't much for to show ee." And away they strode together.

"'Mistress mine'!" repeated Joanne and in such tone that her aunt's gentle though remarkably shrewd eyes twinkled as she murmured:

"Very poetically quaint, my dear!"

"Quaint? Poetical!" repeated Joanne indignantly. "Aunt, what do you think of him?"

"My dear, if you mean your Mr. Anson, I like him."

"He is not 'my' Mr. Anson, Aunt—the idea! And I'm not sure that I like him one bit! He is quite too pertinaciously familiar—and, besides, there is some mystery about him, something almost—furtive——"

"Goodness, child! Are you suggesting he is a malefactor, a runaway jail-bird, an escaped convict, a——"

"Aunt Jemima! What an atrociously abominable idea! All I meant was that he is so—so unexpected, so utterly different to any other man I ever met."

"Well, they say originality is divine. Where did you meet him?"

"Outside Joe Todger's nasty little alehouse with a tankard in his hand."

"Ah, you mean he is a wine and ale bibber, a drunkard——"

"No—I—do—not! I didn't see him drink——"

"Ah," sighed Aunt Jemima, smiling down at her busy rolling-pin, "a secret drinker, which is worse—though I didn't think he looked a criminal type."

"Of course he isn't!" said Joanne, glancing indignantly at the back of Aunt Jemima's carefully averted head.

"Then, my dear, why this nonsense about his being furtive and mysterious?"

"Because he is. When first I saw him he was——"

"Guzzling ale, you say."

"No! I said there was a tankard——"

"From which he guzzled!"

"Nothing of the kind, Aunt—though Bill said he was perishing with thirst. No, what struck me was his appearance. He looked so hot and tired and fearfully dusty that I knew he must have travelled a long way and evidently on foot——"

"But, my dear, he does not look a common tramp."

"Certainly not, Aunt! Yet why should he trudge afoot in such heat and dust?"

"Perhaps he is poor, a needy gentleman who has seen better days. For a gentleman he is, Joanne!"

"So I think, Aunt. But why tramp the roads? And why to our village? And why lodge at Will Lawler's Soaring Lark? And why work for me for mere pittance?"

"Why don't you ask him, my dear?"

"I mean to—when I know him better—perhaps."

Meanwhile Nicholas, in shirt-sleeves and armed with the necessary tools, was surveying all that remained of the ancient barn's massive door, whereat Bill shook solemn head, saying:

"A praper old ruination it be, sir, sure-ly!"

"Yet what there is of it is good old English oak, Bill, and pretty sound. A brace of stout battens with three or four planks should make it do for the time being."

The timber being produced, Nicholas got to work with saw and adze, chisel and hammer, and, thus busied, was whistling blithely, when he became aware of a supremely elegant horseman approaching, a handsome, youthful-seeming person, who, on closer inspection, proved older than was at first apparent; an arrogant, bold-eyed person, who, reining in his spirited horse, cried in the tone of one used to implicit and instant obedience:

"Hi, you there, drop that hammer and come and hold my horse!"

"Certainly, sir, if you'll drop your horse and hold my hammer."

"Eh—what—what?" exclaimed the person, with threatening gesture of his hunting-crop. "Now, damme, but I believe you are trying to be insolent."

"And be damned to you, sir, if I'm not succeeding!" The person wheeled his trampling horse and raised the hunting-crop. Nicholas stepped forward, twirling his heavy hammer. Then was flutter of petticoats and Joanne was between them.

"Whatever are you doing?" she demanded.

"This—this fellow——" stuttered the person.

"Is my—is a Mr. Anson," she said rather breathlessly. "Mr. Anson, this—this is Charles, Lord Wolverton."

"This impudent fellow actually affronted me, Joanne!"

"This very lordly fellow actually bellowed at me, marm. He would also actually have interfered with my work and since that work is for Mistress Joanne, no lord alive is going to let or stay me, actually."

"Then, Charles—my lord, I will not allow you, or anyone else, to interfere with my—my—workpeople."

Beneath scowling brow my lord inserted an eyeglass the better to glare on Anthony, saying:

"Joanne, I merely asked your labourer fellow to hold my horse!"

"He is far better occupied, Charles! Which makes me wonder why your horse is here?"

"I rode over, for one thing, to discuss Harbourne's amazing conduct—this lowering of rents, this——"

"Yes," she sighed, "it is indeed amazing, and——"

"It's infinitely worse, Joanne! It's betrayal of his class, of us! It's a direct incitement to revolt! The whole rural community will be dissatisfied with their lot——"

"No, with their little, Charles, and no wonder! I have often thought they are shamefully underpaid."

"But damme, Jo, don't you see——"

"Do—not—swear, my lord!"

"No—forgive me! But don't you see the danger this fool Harbourne is causing?"

"No! I see and hear around me lately only happiness, smiling faces and glad voices instead of gloom and misery."

"And I'm telling you, Joanne, Harbourne's madness is a direct incitement to revolution, rebellion, and probably civil war! The fellow is an accursed menace."

"No, Charles, he is such a public blessing that I should like to go on my knees to him."

"Eh? Should you, b'gad?"

"I should indeed, but, since I cannot, I pray God's blessing on him instead!"

"On this—this fellow?"

"On this noble-hearted gentleman!"

"Oh, well, no more of him, because I desire to see you on a—more important matter, m'dear."

"I am—not your dear nor ever shall be."

"Are you so sure of this?"

"Perfectly sure—and certain!"

"I wonder! Because, m'dear, I desire a word or two with you—business and so on——"

"Oh . . . business?" she repeated distressfully and with such hopeless, weary gesture that Nicholas, about to use his hammer, rubbed his shaven chin with it instead and knit his brow in angry perplexity.

"So shall we go indoors, m'dear?"

"Oh, if you must. But Aunt Jemima shall hear you as well."

"As you please. Though you are mistress here——"

"Yes, but for how long?"

"This all depends on you, m'dearest; you have only to say——"

"I never shall, Charles, never——"

"Circumstances may compel you to——"

"I shall defy them and—oh, come to the house and Aunt Jemima."

Having watched them out of sight, Nicholas scowled at his hammer, shook his head at it and fell to work again, but presently to him came Bill with his two fellow labourers, a rather self-conscious Bill, who, touching his hat, said:

"Mist' Anson, sir, since now you be one o' we and b'long like, I rackon as how ee should ought to know these yere chaps as 'ave b'longed at Fallowdenes' many years."

"Good for them!" said Nicholas heartily. "I should like to shake their hands."

"So ee shall, sir, but first lemme do things praper. This," said he, clapping the broad shoulder of a stalwart shy-grinning fellow, "this be Jarge as won ploughin'-match last year. And this old un be Joe, the cowman, as should ought to be dead and buried years ago but do choose to be alive and work for Mistus Joanne. So now, sir, us as was but three is four, so let's shake 'ands all round, sir, if you please." The which Nicholas did forthwith.

All the afternoon he laboured until the fragment of door, though somewhat of a patchwork, was at least a serviceable door again. He was surveying his handiwork rather dubiously, when a soft voice, unexpectedly near, enquired timidly:

"Oh, please, who are you?" Glancing round, he beheld a small, extremely demure feminine person, very prim, from pink sunbonnet to little sandalled feet, who, looking up at him with large dark eyes, made him a curtsy, slim finger crooked beneath dimpled chin, saying as she did so:

"Please, who are you, I wonder? I'm named Priscilla, though sometimes I'm called 'Pris', and I don't like it because it's so hissy. So please what's your name?"

"Priscilla is a very pretty name," said he, smiling, "and you may call me Anthony."

"Well, Anthony's a pretty name, too, like the call of a bird."

"A bird, sweetheart?"

"Yes, in a wood when it calls good night—like this: An—too—nee. Have you been mending this poor old door?"

"Yes, what do you think of it, Priscilla?"

"You must be a fright-flee clever sort of Anthony to make it so nice and strong again, only it wants to be painted."

"It does, my dear, and it shall be."

"Nice darky-green, Anthony, like trees look at evening. I love trees, don't you?"

"So much, sweetheart, that I hate to see them cut down!"

"So do I, 'cause it takes them such a long time and so much trouble to grow themselves nice and big, doesn't it?"

"Yes, my dear, and such a short time to fell them. And yet we must have wood to build our houses and ships and things."

"And I like ships, too, with their lovely white sails."

"Yes, a ship is a wonderful and beautiful thing, Priscilla."

"Frogs are lovely, too, Anthony, when they're little. I have one here in the pocket of my pinafore what looks at me with golden eyes. I'll show you." Here, after some groping, she extracted the frog, holding it out on small, pink palm, which little creature seemed to regard them and the universe in general with eyes like jewels.

"There, Anthony, isn't he lov——" Here, with sudden tremendous leap, this small frog vanished in the grass which grew thickly nearby.

"Oh well," sighed Priscilla, "perhaps he's better where he b'longs. So now, if you like, I'll give you first bite of my apple," and from that same pocket she drew the fruit in question, saying: "One side's a bit green, so you'd better try the pinky part."

"Thank you, sweetheart," said he very tenderly, "but I don't feel apple-ish just at present."

"And I don't, too," said she, dropping it back into her pocket. "But I do like the way you call me 'sweetheart'! Does it mean that you love me?"

"It certainly does, Priscilla!"

"Oh, but that's a bit quicky soon, isn't it? 'Cause our Ann what's going to marry our George told Polly our dairymaid as how she didn't allow him to call her 'sweetheart' till they'd walked out a month."

At this moment Lord Wolverton approached at leisured trot and his youthful-seeming face showed grim, also he reined his horse to a walk the better to scowl down on Nicholas, seemed about to speak, but, meeting the child's wide gaze, spurred his horse viciously and rode away at a gallop.

"That," said little Priscilla, gazing after him, "was a lord and very rich, but I don't like him; do you?"

"The place is lovelier without him, sweetheart."

"Yes, it is—lots! But he often comes riding here 'cause our Nancy says he wants to take my Auntie Joanne in wedlock's holy bonds; and sometimes after he's gone, she—I mean Auntie Jo—sheds tears, weeps, you know, and Aunt Jemima looks as if she would, too."

"Does she, my dear?"

"Yes, and I can't think why, unless it's the way he looks at her with his eyeglass that glitters so twinkly. . . . Oh, there's Ann ringing the tea bell, so come along!"

"Oh, but, dear heart," said he, "I'm not expected or invited—and, besides, I'm not fit to sit down at any lady's dainty tea-table."

"Yes, you are a rather grubby Anthony, but you can dust yourself and wash your hands at the pump over there. I'll wag the handle for you. . . . Oh, there's Auntie now to take me in to tea! Auntie Jo!" she called in her sweet young voice. "I've told Anthony to wash his hands and come in to tea, but he's being disobedient to me."

"So, miss, you call him 'Anthony', do you——"

"Yes, because, Auntie, he calls me 'sweetheart' and says he loves me, and so do I."

"Good gracious, child, what are you saying?"

"The truth, Miss Joanne, the sweet and simple truth, for who wouldn't love her?"

"So please, Auntie Jo, tell him to wash his hands and come in to tea."

"Oh, but, Priscilla," Nicholas demurred, "indeed, Miss Joanne, I——"

"Had better obey your imperious sweetheart, sir; so wash your hands instantly and come to tea. And let me thank you, Mr. Anson, for the barn door; it should last now for years. You are indeed a handyman and, with my admiring gratitude, have earned your tea."

Thus presently, in spacious panelled chamber, its great beams carved richly as the wide over-mantel, and with wide lattices open to the fragrant garden, down they sat to well-laden table, with Aunt Jemima to preside at the tea-pot, a large cameo brooch in the lace at her throat, a belaced cap upon her grey hair, gentle-eyed and serene. So cups and saucers chinked (sweet homely sound); Joanne talked rather perfunctorily of cows, sheep, and her hopes for the coming harvest, sipped her tea,

D

and, eating nothing, sighed instead, at which times Nicholas glanced at her in vague and puzzled anxiety, while Aunt Jemima, serene yet keen of eye, watched them both, until Priscilla, setting down her cup with a clatter, announced:

"Anthony doesn't like Lord Wolverton like we don't, but he does like frogs, so I like him lots and lots, because I'm his sweetheart; and so, Anthony, after tea will you please help me with my homework, three nasty, long sums, and I hate 'rithmetick, so will you please, Anthony?"

"No," said Joanne, roused from some troubled thought, "you must not trouble Mr. Anson with your sums; I will help you."

"No thank you, Auntie Jo; last time you got one wrong. So will you, Anthony?"

"You should say Mr. Anthony, child, or Mr. Anson would be more polite!"

"Please, no!" said Nicholas. "Priscilla and I don't have to bother with politeness."

"Pray," said Aunt Jemima, as she refilled his cup, "pray, Mr. Anson, do you happen to know Lord Wolverton."

"No, ma'm, I do not!"

"Yet you do not like him."

"He is a gentleman I prefer—at a distance."

"May I know the reason for your dislike?"

"Miss Jemima, I can only answer by quoting that aged rhyme:

'I do not like thee, Doctor Fell,
The reason why I cannot tell,

But this I know, and know full well,
I—do—not like thee, Doctor Fell.' "

"Do you know if he is acquainted with our dearly beloved benefactor, Sir Nicholas Harbourne?"

"Miss Jemima, I—cannot say. Why do you ask?"

"Because Lord Wolverton, who is often in London and seems to know everyone of any consequence, assures us that Sir Nicholas is a young man."

"Which," declared Joanne, cup at ruddy lip, "I shall never believe, especially on the word of Charles! No! I am quite convinced our dear Sir Nicholas is an aged gentleman tottering gravewards—upon his last legs and a stick or probably crutches, who, knowing he cannot live much longer, has given all this money to his tenants rather than leave it to some detested relative or public institution. This perfectly explains his conduct. And just because he is so stricken in years, and therefore wise enough to be so nobly generous, I love him and always shall!"

"And what say you, Mr. Anson?"

"Miss Jemima, I am wondering if Miss Joanne could and would love this gentleman should he prove to be indeed a young man?"

"Well, Joanne?"

"Aunt, the question does not arise, because I am quite certain the dear old gentleman is on the very brink of his grave. Ah, but his noble deed will endure long after him, to bless his people and keep his dear memory forever green and living."

The meal ending, Nicholas rose to bow and say fervently:

"Ladies, for your so kind hospitality to a lonely fellow I am profoundly grateful——"

"And to me, too, Anthony?" Priscilla enquired wistfully.

"To you, my dear one," he answered, setting his arm about her small form, "ever and always."

"Then now will you help me with my nasty 'rithmetick?"

"Of course, if your aunt will allow."

This permission accorded, down sat Nicholas, with Priscilla beside him, and together the three sums were worked out.

Thereafter, as evening fell, Priscilla, unwilling but obedient, kissed them all three and sped lightly upstairs to bed. . . .

Now it happened that as Anthony strolled homewards through a fragrant twilight he was accosted by old Mrs. Mills, who, grasping his sleeve in one labour-gnarled hand, fumbled a crumpled paper from the pocket of her apron with the other, a paper printed in extremely bold characters, saying:

"Young man, will ee please to read me this yere, for I bean't much of a scholard and there be words as I don't nowise understand, and them as I do seems too wunnerful for me to b'lieve."

So, taking this paper, Nicholas read aloud:

" 'To Mrs. Rebecca Mills. Madam, On and after June Sixth proximo, the messuage known as Mills Cot, together with the land adjacent thereto, being three acres and one rod, becomes your sole property to have and to hold in perpetuity. By order.' "

"Oh merciful Lord!" she whispered, then, giving a fierce tug at the sleeve she clutched, demanded: "That word 'per-pit-tooity'—what do it mean?"

"That your cottage is really yours, for ever and ever, Mrs. Mills."

"Mine?" she whispered. "For ever and ever! To 'ave and to 'old! 'Twas like as parson said when my dear Tom wed me s'long ago! To 'ave and to 'old for ever and ever! And I d' hear tell as 'tis arl by order o' Sir Nich'las 'Arbourne . . . to have and hold t' the end o' my days. . . ."

The harsh old face became wonderfully transfigured, the fierce old eyes were softened by slow-gathering tears, and, in voice altered as her look, she murmured:

"Oh, please gimme that precious paper; thankee kindly! I be agoing to keep it in my old Bible where my Tom writ the names and birthdays of our three dear sons. Ah, and I be agoing to pray again for to thank the dear Lord God for such mercy and His blessing on Sir Nich'las 'Arbourne."

Then, with the paper folded reverently between her work-roughened hands, Mrs. Mills bowed her white head and, with a great sob of rapturous gladness, hobbled away.

CHAPTER VII

Concerning Hobnailed Boots and the Magic of Cards

WITH Bill, shaved and suitably attired, beside her in the gig, Joanne had driven to market, and Aunt Jemima, seated beside the open lattice, was, for once, neither sewing, knitting, crocheting nor talking; instead she was deeply engaged upon a game of patience which stubbornly refused to come out.

"Drat the cards!" she exclaimed, albeit gently and perfectly serene of face. "Oh, drat the hateful things!" she murmured, in which moment, chancing to glance up, she espied Anthony in shirt-sleeves, but opened her gentle eyes rather wider than usual and, leaning from the casement, exclaimed: "Good gracious!" because from hobnailed boots and thick, buttoned gaiters to the vivid bandanna neckerchief about his throat, Anthony was clad as any self-respecting farmhand should or possibly could be.

Perceiving her astonishment, he laughed blithely, saying:

"Being now Mistus Joanne's handyman and labourer-in-general, marm, I thought it right to dress for the part."

"You have indeed!" said Aunt Jemima, laughing also. "Has Joanne seen you?"

"Not yet."

"I wonder whatever she will say?"

"So do I!" he chuckled.

"Well now, are you particularly busy, Mr. Anthony?"

"Not particularly, Miss Jemima."

"Oh, pray forgive my calling you Mr. Anthony—so familiar—but ever since she met you last week Priscilla has so chattered of her 'Anthony' that as 'Anthony' I think of you, Mr. Anson."

"Oh, please do!" said he, almost eagerly. "I love the idea and should love it even more if you would drop the 'mister'."

"So I will, Anthony, if you'll agree to cease 'miss-ing' me and call me Aunt Jemima."

"Indeed I'd love to do so."

"Then, Anthony, let us be aunt and nephew—by adoption."

"Dear Aunt Jemima, you honour me so greatly that—well, I cannot express my gratitude——"

"Then please don't try; tell me instead if you ever play any of these very annoying patience games."

"Frequently, Aunt. And, as your nephew, I must confess I lived by the cards at one time in my chequered career."

"But is not that a very uncertain way of earning a livelihood?"

"Not when one knows how to play. For, Aunt Jemima, I was a manipulator, a prestigiator."

"Goodness me! Whatever was that?"

"A card-sharper, Aunt."

"Anthony!" she exclaimed, gently horrified. "You do not, you cannot mean a—cheat?"

"I do indeed. But I only cheated when I saw others were cheating me. Then I proceeded to out-sharp the sharpers."

"But how could you?"

"In many ways. I was taught the craft by a great master of the art with magic in his every finger. I became his pupil and partner, and we did extremely well until he died in far Western America, at a place called Bannock, in the street one night and very suddenly."

"Ah, poor man! Was it a stroke?"

"Yes, Aunt, of a bowie-knife—in the back."

"Oh, Anthony, how dreadful! Was the cowardly murderer ever caught and brought to justice?"

"He was—I squared the account."

"You don't mean—you—oh, do you mean——"

"Dear Aunt Jemima, Jake had been my friend and, apart from cards, was a simple, kindly soul, and in those days Bannock and thereabouts knew no law except knife and gun. So when poor old Jake was gone I quit the game and returned to sea, and should be there now, but for—well—circumstances quite unforeseen and wholly unexpected. So that is the story of your nephew. I do hope it has not shocked you, dear Aunt Jemima."

"Oh, but it has! It is a most horrid and very dreadful story—Nephew!"

"Life can be both, sometimes!" he sighed. "Have I shocked you so much that you wish to un-adopt me?"

"No, my—my dear!" she replied with rather a quavery laugh. "But my life has always been so sheltered and uneventful, and yours so very stormy, it seems."

"Yes," he answered gloomily, "on sea and land! This is why life here . . . the gentle loveliness of you all is so infinitely precious to me, and the fear that some day I may lose it . . . be compelled to leave it is a thought so bitterly distressing that——"

"Then don't think such a thought, my dear, and, to banish such nonsense, tell me, is there magic still in your fingers, Anthony?"

"I believe so, Aunt, though they are probably rather clumsy from lack of constant practice."

"Could you perform card tricks?"

"My dear, of course."

"Then come in at once and show me some. This moment, Nephew, through the window and never mind your horrid nailed boots."

Laughing now, in he came and, taking up the pack of cards, riffled them swiftly through his long sinewy fingers, saying as he did so:

"Dearest of aunts, from these fifty-two pasteboards your dutiful nephew chooses one card, to him lovelier than all the rest—watch now!" Speaking, he tossed the pack into the air and, as the cards scattered and fell, snatched one and showed the Queen of Hearts, saying: "Here she is, bless her!" and, speaking, he touched the card with his lips.

"How wonderful!" cried Aunt Jemima, for once forgetting her serenity. "But could you do it again?"

"As often as you wish!" he answered, and, sweeping the fallen cards together, tossed, scattered them, and from the air plucked again the Queen of Hearts. Then, before she could utter a word, he collected, shuffled, spread them into a fan and proffered them to her. "Now, my dear, select any one you prefer."

And after deliberating on her choice, she drew a card, turned it and saw she herself was now holding this most persistent Queen of Hearts; and after she had insisted upon making three more attempts and always with the same result, Aunt Jemima, sinking back in her chair, gazed up at him in such awed bewilderment that, urged by sudden impulse, he stooped to kiss her perplexed brow, saying very tenderly:

"Oh, Aunt Jemima dear, sweet innocent, these are merely the very simplest tricks."

And so, at her eager request and to her ever-growing wonder, he showed her those marvels of dexterity with cards few and many, such as only skilled hands may perform: cards that vanished and reappeared; cards that seemed to change themselves even as she watched; cards that flew spinning through the air from one hand to return, like homing pigeons, to the other; cards that seemed to obey his every word and gesture, until, shaping them into a pack, he ventured once again to kiss her.

"Well, Anthony," said she a little breathlessly, "now that we have become so—so very suddenly familiar—and I like it—I demand to know why you make so very much of the Queen of Hearts and why you blessed and kissed her."

"Aunt Jemima," he replied gravely, "though I think you have guessed already, it is because—throned in my heart is Joanne, to be loved and honoured more reverently and truly than any queen. This is why I told you something of my rather ugly past—that you might judge of my worthiness and—oh, my dear, I beg you to be—merciful, as you can."

Here again Miss Jemima leant back in her chair to scan his every feature: the square brow, black-lashed eyes, wide, sensitive mouth, aquiline nose and almost too aggressive line of jaw and chin. "A handsome face? No, but very nearly! A strong face? Yes, most decidedly! A good face?" Aunt Jemima, eyes keenly intent, was silent so long that he became restless at last, yet his grey eyes never wavered, but his tone was very wistful as he enquired gently:

"Is it 'No', my dear?" And as gently she answered:

"Nephew Anthony, you may kiss your aunt again."

CHAPTER VIII

*How Nicholas Glimpsed the Shadow Again—with the
Reason Therefor*

RETURNING from market this same afternoon, Joanne
was surprised to behold a strange-seeming man plying a
pitchfork (and very clumsily) on a pile of stable sweepings.

"Who are you?" she demanded. The man turned to
knuckle an eyebrow, saying:

" 'Tes only me, mistus."

"Oh, good gracious heavens!" she exclaimed. "What a
spectacle you have made of yourself. Your only mistake
is your too clean-shaven chin."

"Thankee, marm; I'll mind me o' this tomorrer."

"Oh, Mr. Anson, how ridiculous you are!" said she,
frowning, yet smiling also. "Why make such a—an odd-
ment of yourself? Those awful boots! That frightful
thing round your neck! Why?"

"Mistress mine," he said, leaning upon the misused
pitchfork, "I suggest you ask my dear Aunt Jemima."

"Your aunt, indeed!"

"By her most gracious adoption! Wherefore I aver
there is no handyman or farm hand in all Sussex prouder
or happier than yours, Miss Joanne."

Here, before she could find adequate retort, Priscilla
sped towards them, hair and sunbonnet flying as she
uttered her welcoming cry of:

"An—toe—nee!" Down went pitchfork, and next moment she was throned upon his shoulder, in which posture she stooped to kiss his dark head, saying: "Today it's jogafree; all the towns and rivers and all I know is London and the Thames, and Horsham and Harbourne, ten sixty-six, and the cruel arrow in poor King Harold's eye, so will you help me after tea?"

"If your Auntie Joanne will allow——"

"Have you no word of greeting for me?" Joanne enquired, and Nicholas saw her eyes were troubled again with far more than the child's forgetfulness.

"Yes, Aunt Jo, I'll kiss you, too, if you'll please come near enough." But instead Joanne turned away abruptly, saying (and surely the trouble was in her voice also): "I expect tea will be ready, thank goodness."

"Very well, Auntie dear, so when I've pumped my Anthony's hands clean I'll bring him."

"Thank you, sweetheart, but not without your Aunt Joanne's permission."

"But, Mr. Anson, why bother about me? I expect your Aunt Jemima will be expecting you." Then she sped away, leaving Nicholas gazing after her so anxiously that Priscilla patted his head with small, comforting hand.

"I ax-pect," she suggested, "Auntie Jo didn't quite like your nice new boots so big and naily, or this lovely thing round your neck so red as fire, but I do. So come 'long and let's pump."

But when they were seated at the dainty tea-table it seemed to Nicholas there was a shadow all about them despite the sunset glory flooding in through the open casement; also he noticed that Joanne ate nothing, spoke seldom, that her troubled eyes avoided his, and he wondered, until, like a blow, the truth struck him—she had been crying again, and very recently. He glanced helplessly at Aunt Jemima, looked anxiously at Joanne, and at last ventured to enquire very gently:

"Miss Joanne, please can I help you—in any way?"

"No—no, thank you," she replied dully. "No one can help me except myself, and I—will not—oh—never!" Then, upstarting, was gone.

"There," said Priscilla, "I ax-pect she's gone upstairs with a headache 'cause she was crying so tear-fly in the dairy—and when I tried to comfort her like a nice person should, all she said was, 'Go away, child'—so I go-ed."

"Well now—I—wonder!" sighed Aunt Jemima.

"So do I!" said Nicholas. "I'm wondering if you—will allow me the great privilege of knowing precisely what you are wondering, and why? Will you so honour me, Aunt?"

And after brief hesitation:

"Priscilla," said she, gentle of eye but serenely commanding, "take your sampler into the kitchen, my dear, and ask Ann to show you that cross-stitch. And please tell Rose and Nancy that I don't wish them to remove the tea-things until I ring. Go, my dear." And obedient to that command, Priscilla rose, curtsied demurely and departed.

"Well, Anthony, the story I will confide to you is one, oddly enough, concerning cards, the devil's pictures, the evil folly of them! They were my brother Edward's curse, and now, in a way, ours also. Towards the end of his life my poor brother became an inveterate, and at last a desperate, gambler; in one night's play he lost all he possessed, and, besides this, gave Lord Wolverton his I.O.U. for the dreadful sum of twelve thousand five hundred pounds!"

"Was Lord Wolverton the only winner?"

"I am not sure, but today he holds this dreadful I.O.U."

"However, gambling debts are not recoverable by law, Aunt."

"We know it, but Joanne is so proud that she deems this a debt of honour and has been trying to save every possible penny hoping to pay——"

"Is Lord Wolverton asking for or expecting payment?"

"He has been very considerate and forbearing with us as with my poor brother, though he has mentioned this debt lately."

"And so," said Anthony, chin rather more aggressive than usual, "the shadow on Fallowdene, the reason of Joanne's tears, is Wolverton. Well, now and hereafter, damn and curse the fellow!"

"Anthony! My dear! I ought to be shocked—and I suppose I am, but, all things considered, I thank you most gratefully for saying it for me so exceedingly well."

"However, Aunt, something should be done about it."

"Something certainly should, but what?"

"Aunt," replied Anthony, with sudden, grim smile, "pray remember I am your devoted nephew and Joanne's adoring handyman."

"Well, Nephew Anthony, well?"

"Dear Aunt Jemima," said he, as they rose to say goodbye, "I hope and believe it will be."

"Will be what, Nephew, what, pray?"

Nicholas merely smiled and kissed her; but as he strode towards the Soaring Lark that jaw of his showed more aggressive than ever, until, entering this cosy inn, he was greeted by Mrs. Lawler, who curtsied, saying:

"There be only jugged 'are, sir, but wi' a glass or so o' port wine to rich it up a bit."

CHAPTER IX

Of Brutality and a Bull

ANTHONY was busied in the great old tithe-barn reinforcing some of its aged timbers, when he heard a sudden wrangle of angry voices, being those of Bill, George and old Joe, with one other louder, fiercer than all—a deep, harsh voice that bellowed:

"Where's your damn mistress? Let me to her! Go fetch her or I'll set about the three o' ye!"

"Don't ee, sir," said Bill, "or I'll tickle ee wi' me pitchfork, woeful!"

"An' I'll try a clout at ee wi' me fist-es!" growled George.

"And I'll tek a chop at ee wi' me 'o'!" piped old Joe.

But fierce as ever the strange voice bellowed:

"Go bring me your mistress and be cursed t' ye! I say her damn horses ha' broke down my noo fence and she's going to look at it, ay, and pay for it! So fetch her here to me or——"

"Easy all!" said Nicholas, and, stepping from the barn, beheld the devoted three fronting Ferocity in shape of a powerful, bearded man, red of face, fierce of eye, who flourished a walking-stick like a cudgel and demanded:

"Who the devil are you?"

And in the vernacular Nicholas answered:

"I be only the 'andyman, but so 'andy I be as I be now tellin' ee to pipe down and sing small, Whiskers! I be tellin' ee to sheer off and get ee back t' your dunghill—be off, I says, and go along afore I handle and hurt ee!"

"Hold your cursed tongue!" roared Ferocity. "I'm Jem Mason, I am, and can lick any man in Sussex."

"Not with that beard to grapple ye by!" quoth Nicholas with taunting leer. "Wi' such a holdfast, any chap could shake y'r damn ugly head off, ar—no question. So if——"

Ferocity leapt and smote empty air, as, eluding this expected blow, Nicholas closed and, seizing the beard, shook Mr. Mason thereby, this way and that, with a joyous violence, then, releasing Mr. Mason, smote the beard with fist so accurate and powerful that Mr. Mason went over backwards, to lie outstretched and groaning.

"That," laughed Nicholas, "was a right upper-cut, Mr. Mason, which I enjoyed bestowing. So when you've rested sufficiently pray stand up and afford me further pleasure though, damme, I've handled far tougher brutes than you, ashore and afloat. Come, get up, or must I kick you afoot?"

"Don't!" cried a beloved though breathless voice, and Joanne came running. "Oh, how—how can you—be such a brute?" she panted, with eyes for no one and no thing except her very "Handyman". "How can you?"

"Very easily, I'm afraid!" he answered, seeing now only his "mistus".

"You are quite—quite brutal!"

"Mebbeso, marm, but only when by brutality compelled thereto."

"But you . . . Oh, you . . . enjoyed it! I could see you did!"

"I do confess it, mistress mine, though——"

"Do—not—call me—that!"

"Very good, marm. Though I be your man sure-ly same like as friend Bill and Jarge and Joe be—ar no question!"

Here Ferocity, now tamed, and being also protected by Joanne's shapely self, ventured to sit up, groaning so piteously that she turned to bend over him, enquiring anxiously:

"Oh, poor Mr. Mason! Has he hurt you very much?"

"Ay, Miss Marsden, I do believe as your murderous fellow has broke my jaw."

"Oh, I do hope not! Whatever shall I do——"

"Stand ee aside, marm," said Nicholas, doing his best again with the vernacular; "back with ee, marm, and lemme get me fingers in that theer beard."

Mr. Mason arose with surprising nimbleness and, retreating behind Joanne, declared:

"I'll have the law on ye all for this; 'tes a case of murderous assault and battery!"

"Not it, oh no!" growled Nicholas. "'Tes a case of trespass wi' violence! So, Mr. Mason, take that theer beard away prompt—afore I have another go at it, for, d'ye see, me fingers be fair itching for it."

Beholding which clutching fingers, Mr. Mason departed, breathing dire threats, growing louder and fiercer with every stride, but leaving his stick behind, which weapon Nicholas, with an effort, snapped beneath his ponderous hobnailed boot.

"Oh, you shouldn't!" cried Joanne. "The frightful wretch may come back to claim it."

"Not likely, I'm afraid," sighed Nicholas; "but if he only will, he shall have the pieces where he will feel them most."

"He is a dreadful man," Joanne admitted, "almost as fierce as you are, Mr. Anson, but——"

"Marm, the name be Anthony, Tony for short, if you please. And as for Mr. Mason——"

"He was a fighting man once—Mr. Anson."

"Ar, so 'e were!" quoth Bill.

"In the ring," added George, "gloves or bare fist-es——"

"I seen 'im fight once!" piped old Joe.

"Consequently, Mr. Anson, no one dares to—to tackle him single-handed."

"'Cept Mist' Anthony!" chuckled Bill.

"Ar!" quoth George. "Mist' Anthony 'andled 'im so sweet and proper I relished it."

"Ay," piped old Joe, "so lovely 'twere for to see, till you comes 'long, Miss Jo, and sp'iles it."

"Yes, Joe, but only just in time to save the poor hateful wretch from Mr. Anson's great, nailed boots! You were going to kick the beast; confess it—Mr. Anson."

"Though very tenderly, mistress mi——"

"Bill," she demanded, almost stridently, "why was he here? What did he want?"

"Mistus, 'e comes abellering so loud as any old bull and says as 'ow our 'osses 'ad broke 'is noo fence——"

"Which," added George, "couldn't nowise be——"

"Seein' as 'ow," piped old Joe, "they 'osses was in paddock, Miss Jo."

"Thank heaven!" she sighed.

"I d' rackon," said Bill, "the critter as bruk Mr. Mason's fence were that noo young bull as 'e bought last wick."

Now at this moment from the nearby meadow rose a shrill scream, and, glancing thitherward, they beheld little Priscilla pursued by the animal in question, which oncoming, sharp-horned terror seemed gaining upon her with every stride; and as she fled this galloping Death she screamed again and more breathlessly:

"An—toe—nee——" But he was already speeding towards her, and very fleetly, across stable-yard, through the paddock and across shady lane to vault the stile, and with undiminished speed raced on until Priscilla's little, desperate hands were clutching him, his arm about her and the bull thundering towards them. Thus Anthony waited its coming—nearer, nearer yet, until he could not miss. Then, catching up Priscilla beneath his arm, he hurled that devoted hat of his and with aim so true that the bull, thus suddenly blinded for the moment, checked and, as Anthony leapt aside, swerved, shook off the hat and now, forgetful of all else, gored it fiercely, tossing aloft great clouds of earth.

So Anthony bore the child to safety, where Joanne, breathless, pale as death, waited with arms outstretched. And now came Bill with George and old Joe, all variously armed and eager to wreak vengeance on the animal which had so shocked them all. But Anthony, laughing rather shakily, pointed them where the bull now ambled peacefully away, with what had once been a hat impaled upon one murderous horn.

Then Joanne, still half dazed by the suddenness and

horror of what might have been, said and still breathlessly:

"Priscilla wants—her Anthony—Anthony."

So he took the child to his breast, there to kiss and cherish her, saying cheerfully:

"You are all right now, sweetheart."

"Yes," she answered, clinging to him, "'cause you've got me nice and safe 'stead of the bull what you frightened away. So now, if you please, my Anthony, I want me on your shoulder."

"And," sighed Joanne, "she ought to go to bed until teatime after such dreadful shock."

"Right!" said he. "So to bed you must go, sweetheart."

"Oh, but, Anthony, bed's such a stuffy place in the daytime! So now ride me on your shoulder."

"I'd love to, but not until you promise your dear Joanne to lie down and sleep a while like the good, sweet little Priscilla you are."

"Oh, very well, if you'll ride me up to bed on your shoulder, my Anthony."

So with her thus throned, indoors he went, to follow Joanne up the wide, old stair and thus presently into a spacious, fragrant chamber which he knew instinctively must be Joanne's. Here, before she could speak the gratitude she found too deep for ready utterance, he kissed Priscilla and hurried away.

CHAPTER X

Chiefly Concerning a Butler of Price, though Priceless

THIS BEING Saturday afternoon and his week's labour finished, Nicholas, hatless, set off villagewards. Reaching the Soaring Lark, he washed, changed into his ordinary though rather shabby garments and went downstairs, to find tea awaiting him, bread and butter, ham, crisp lettuce and a cake "cooked very plain, sir, though with a few curren's, candied peel and a almond or so".

This goodly meal over, Nicholas took his only other hat and sallied forth to see what he might of that so famous and magnificent house called Grayladies.

It was a glorious evening, for old Sol, trending westwards, was doing his best to show off and intensify the beauties of sweeping downland, bowery village and lush countryside, beyond which was a faint, far glory that was the Sussex sea. Moreover, as Nicholas went his leisured way, he sensed in the very air about him an all-pervading gladness. Faces smiled, men hailed one another cheerily, women laughed; from the wide village green rose the merry clamour of children's voices.

"Happiness, sir!" said another voice behind him, and, turning, Nicholas beheld one clad in clerical garb far shabbier than his own garments, a truly gentle man whose somewhat careworn features were for the moment gladdened by a wistful smile, as he repeated: "Happiness, sir, with a huge content! Now and in the future—for all of us hereabouts shall be a glad summer! And the cause of all this, a man who by his one act has done more for my hard-working flock, these simple-hearted honest folk, than I with all my devoted labour and many sermons. Wherefore last Sunday in church I humbly besought God's blessing on their benefactor, Sir Nicholas Harbourne. . . . If your way is mine, may I walk with you, Mr. Anson?"

"With pleasure, sir. But how——"

"Your name? Oh, I know everyone hereabout, being a pastor who tends his flock, and I had mention of you from the gracious ladies at Fallowdene, old and dear friends of mine."

"Were you acquainted with Mr. Edward Marsden?"

"Yes, indeed, and there was a sad case, alas! A gentleman by birth and education, an excellent farmer and extremely well-to-do, until—ruined by the folly of cards! When he died—of remorse, as I believe, poor fellow—he left little but debts, and but for the valiant efforts of those two gentle ladies, aided by the loyal devotion of their three men, William, George and old Joe, they would have lost their loved Fallowdene, that home of the Marsdens for generations. But today, thanks to Joanne's valiant spirit and Miss Jemima's ever serene confidence, they do well enough, God bless them! And, sir, I am glad to learn from Joanne that you are become their handyman."

"She told you this, did she, sir?"

"Yes, Mr. Anson, and with that all too rare laugh of hers. Life has been hard for her and altogether too joyless since her father died."

"Do you know Lord Wolverton, sir?"

"I know—of him, of course; one must, since his property marches with the Harbourne estate."

"Neither do I!" said Nicholas, pausing where the ways divided.

"What, pray, Mr. Anson?"

"Like the fellow."

Then they smiled, bowed to one another, shook hands with sudden fervour, and went their ways, the devoted parson to his unending duties, while Nicholas ambled on towards that noble edifice called Grayladies.

Reaching the ponderous iron gates at last, he found them closed, tugged the iron handle of a bell suspended nearby, until at last a man appeared, who merely frowned, shook his head and vanished again. So Nicholas reached for the bell again, but checked the impulse and instead followed the course of a singularly forbidding wall until he found a place where the ground rose sufficiently for him to reach the top of this grim obstruction; then, swinging himself lightly aloft, over he went and down. Around him were spacious gardens, smoothly mown lawns, a glory of flowers, well-trimmed hedges, leafy bowers whence marble fauns and dryads peeped, while before him rose the great house throned in glory upon its three terraces, a stately monument of many epochs, stone, brick, timber and plaster welded together into one magnificent structure and this mellowed by centuries of time.

Gazing up at this truly imposing edifice, Nicholas approached and slowly mounted the wide, marble steps leading from one terrace to another until he reached the third and last, and now, approaching the house itself, was peering through one of the very many windows, when a voice huskily suggestive of choice wines and richly seasoned meats cried in oily though commanding tone:

"Young man—forbear!"

Glancing round, Nicholas espied a superbly dignified personage altogether remarkable though chiefly for chins (three), whiskers (fluffy), and waistcoat (spacious, nobly rounded, discreetly obtrusive)—a stately being this, leisured of movement, lofty of mien and so pompously original of speech that Nicholas stood enthralled.

"Young man, be ashamed to peep and to pry upon our privacy! How dare you! What do you? Who are you?"

And, touching his hat respectfully, Nicholas replied:

"I'm nobody in particular. But, oh, sir, pray who can you possibly be, being so preposterously impossible? So, pray, sir, if you are really real, inform me of yourself the who and what and why of you; speak me your name, I beg, that I may attempt to realise your reality."

The Personage (with capital P) blinked large fish-like eyes, smoothed the three chins, cleared the husky voice, and intoned the more richly:

"Young man, in me you be-hold authority, by name James Figgis, ten years butler to the late 'ighly haristo-cratic Sir—Jonas—Harbourne! And, young man, authfor-ity aforesaid bids you to hence yourself—forthwith and—himmediate!"

Nicholas, coughing to hide the laughter that nearly choked him, took off his hat again and bowed, saying humbly:

"Oh, Mr. Figgis, sir, why dismiss me from your

presence just as I begin to appreciate its true grandeur? Why?"

"Young man, I grieve therefore, but dooty being so, so I needs must therefore perform. I dismiss you herefrom because this is no place for you or the commonality in general. Nobility's foot alone must tread these stately pre-sinks! Lordly voices only may wake the echoes of this haristo-cratic 'istorical pile! And by 'pile', young man, I mean far more than mere mansion!"

"Do you really, sir?"

"Ah, I do! All visitations here are discouraged, strangers all forbid and the general public refused entry! Grayladies, young man, is sakry-sank!"

"Is it indeed, sir? May I know why?"

"Because this no-bel eddy-fice has been honoured ere now by royalty, foreign and home-grown, of oom our glorious Elizabethan Queen was one! Wherefore, young man, I bid you now remove. I have con-versed with you longer than I meant or deem proper, considering——"

"Considering what, if you please?"

"That I am oo I am and you of the hoy polloy, and so I bid you begone."

"Suppose I refuse?"

"In that unseemly case, young fellow, I shall summon a brace of my footmen and order same to cast you forth on the common highway where you belong."

"Suppose I offer you a shilling to show me over the place?"

"It is not to be supposed; such piteous proffer would be a most heenious affront."

"A pound, then, a golden sovereign?"

Mr. Figgis thumbed his three chins, gazed dreamily on nothing in particular and murmured:

"Show me!" Nicholas produced the coin. Mr. Figgis, glancing askance, thereon murmured: "Sir, it's a go!" and reached forth a chubby, though clutching hand, from which Nicholas recoiled, exclaiming as in shocked surprise:

"Oh, Mr. Figgis—fie, a bribe! And that you should go so cheaply! One pound will buy you, it seems, and —oh, the shame, the pity of it! Suppose I inform your master——"

"My master? Eh? You mean——"

"Sir Nicholas Harbourne, of course. Suppose I tell him his superb Mr. Figgis, butler extraordinary, is open to bribes?"

"Tell him, sir? 'Oly 'eavens, d'you know Sir Nicholas?"

"Oh yes; we were shipmates for years. I knew him long before he was Sir Nicholas."

"A f-friend o' the master?" gasped Mr. Figgis, mopping at suddenly beaded, care-wrung brow. "The master's friend? Gooramitey, and I called you 'young man'!"

"Also 'young feller'. You, moreover, threatened me with footmen—a brace! I'm mighty sure your master won't approve your treatment of his old friend."

"Cor love a perishing duck!" sighed Mr. Figgis, forgetting all affectations in his dismay and reverting to his original Cockney idiom. "Blimey, here's a go!"

"Aha!" laughed Nicholas, digging thumb into the waistcoat. "That's better, Figgy, for there spake the genuine Fig! So now, as simple man to man——"

"Hush, sir, narra word! Here comes Miss Joanne Marsden, and she's always thought so well of me, so hush, sir, I in-treat!" So saying, Mr. Figgis took off his hat and waved it rather as if it had been the Royal Standard or any other emblem of grandeur.

"So," said Joanne, reining up her mare at foot of the terrace steps and glancing up at Nicholas with very evident surprise, "so then you know each other?"

"Well," answered Nicholas, smiling, "I am just beginning to appreciate Mr. Figgis at his true worth. I came for a glimpse at this enormity called Grayladies, and—well—I'm glimpsing it."

"Isn't it a glory!" She sighed, gazing up at its wide façade. "But I am here today merely to be inquisitive. Mr. Figgis, have you seen or heard anything of our wonderful Sir Nicholas yet? If so, then for mercy's sake be a dear and tell me all you know of him, do!"

"Miss Joanne, I regret to inform you as my answer is in the negaytive. The master to me is yet a mistree and therefore all unbeknown. But this here gentleman can tell us both, him being an old friend o' Sir Nicholas, or leastways so he do give me to understand."

"You?" she cried, her beautiful eyes widening with amazement. "You . . . know Sir . . . Nicholas Harbourne, and you are . . . a friend of his?"

"More or less. We were at sea together, old shipmates, Miss Joanne."

"In Her Gracious Majesty's Royal Navy, sir, of course!"

"No, Mr. Figgis, in the Merchant Marine."

"Sir, I find that a-mazing. Such is hardly the service

for our young haristocrats, sir, the junessy dor-ee of England, hardly, sir—no!"

"Oh well," said Joanne, turning her mare, "Mr. Figgis, I should love you to show me more of the glories of this most glorious place; I didn't see half on my last visit. So will you please, sometime after Harvest-home?"

"Miss Joanne, with abounding joy and a pleasure infinite, and any friends you care to bring along."

"Thank you, Mr. Figgis."

"And I'm glad to see your crops show so very promising, Miss Joanne; a good harvest?"

"Oh, I hope so. But, anyhow, this will be a—a glad summer; I feel it, I know it; yes, a glad and happy summer for many others, too, thanks to Sir Nicholas. Goodbye, Mr. Figgis."

"The same to yourself, Miss Joanne my lady, and I beg you'll remember you are ever welcome here at Grayladies seeing as how."

"As how what, Mr. Figgis?"

"As how you're of The Quality, ah, as beautifully and truly so as any nobel lady oo ever graced a corry-net."

"Oh, Mr. Figgis, you are a perfect lamb and the sweetest of pets. Goodbye!" And with radiant smile she rode away, albeit she reined her spirited mare to an amble and then a walk.

"Fare thee well, Figs!" said Nicholas, prodding the waistcoat again, but this time with a gentle fist that, opening, showed that same golden coin which he thrust into a now unwilling chubby hand, saying:

"That's for your corry-net, Figgy."

CHAPTER XI

How (According to Joanne) Not to Make Love

LONG BEFORE she had reached the great lodge gates, open now, Nicholas was beside her. Graciously she smiled down upon this once sullen lodgekeeper with the enquiry:

"Well, Ben, how is the baby?"

And, touching an eyebrow that no longer scowled, Ben replied:

"Prime, Miss Jo! Famous! So strong as a li'l bull 'e be and 'andsome as a picter. They do say as 'e d' take arter me. My Mary be out wi' un to village or I'd ha' showed 'e to ee."

"Better luck next time, Ben. Give my love to Mary and a kiss to your little Ben."

"I will that, Miss Jo, and thankee kindly. Good arternoon to ee."

Now scarcely were they out upon the sunny, tree-shaded road (dusty, of course) than the smile vanished from Joanne's ruddy lips which did their best to be grim, as, frowning down upon Nicholas, she exclaimed in a tone of bitter reproach, anger and indignation:

"So! You know him! Sir Nicholas Harbourne is your friend! And all these weeks you have not said one single word about him! And why not, I should like to know? No, I demand to know. So why not?"

"Well," he answered, lamely, "why should I?"

"Because all these weeks you have allowed me to deceive myself! You have permitted me to think and talk of him as an old, old man while all the time you knew—how old is he, pray?"

"About thirty-one or so."

"Thirty-one!" she repeated furiously. "And you sat by, dumb as a horrid stock or stone, and allowed me to talk of his 'old white head'. You even suggested he was bald!"

"I don't remember saying so."

"Then you implied it! You allowed me to say how I should love to kiss his dear old wrinkled face, and never uttered a word."

"I was trying to imagine the scene, Joanne."

"Oh, what an idiot, what a perfect fool you must have thought me!"

"No! I thought you lovelier than ever—gentle, tender and perfectly ador——"

"I was a fool, of course, and now I—I'm only too detestably aware of it! Ah, but you, Mr. Anson—I declare you are the most hatefully secretive, furtive and abhorrently sly wretch that ever breathed!"

"Not sly, Joanne——"

"Yes, hatefully, vilely, damnably sly! There, now I've said it, and I'm glad, for so you are!"

"Very well, I am!" he agreed meekly.

"But why—oh why," she wailed, becoming almost tearful, "how could you . . . why did you let me deceive myself so cruelly? Were you afraid or ashamed to own Sir Nicholas as your friend, or what?"

"No, I hated to destroy your picture of him."

"Which was entirely wrong! Wrinkles, snow-white hair, a bowed and tottery form—and he—only thirty-one! Mr. Anson, you are a beast!"

"But a very gentle, faithful beast, Joanne?"

"What is he really like?"

"A rather ordinary sort of fellow."

"He is nothing of the kind! No ordinary man could have behaved to his poor folk as he has done! Oh no; now that my eyes are opened you shall not blind me—this would be heaping cruelty upon all your sly, wilfully deceiving reticence! And you are not quite mercilessly cruel, are you?"

"I hope not."

"Very well, then! Now try your best to be frank, open, aboveboard and tell me what he is like—his appearance and in plain words."

"Fairly plain——"

"Do—not—be silly! Tell me, is he dark or fair, tall or short?"

"Fairishly dark and tallish."

"Is he good-looking? He is, of course, he must be, but what I mean is—is he handsome?"

"So remarkably so, Miss Jo, that it is generally remarked."

"Oh . . . indeed?" said she, eyeing him very dubiously.

"Indeed, yes!" replied Nicholas, warming to his theme. "The gentler sex set so many caps, hats and bonnets at him that he ran away to sea to escape the——"

"Mr. Anson," said she, gathering up her reins, "I have told you already that you are a beast——"

F

"And I, Joanne, described your beast as faithful and——"

"Can you and will you at least tell me this—does Sir Nicholas intend to live at Grayladies?"

"No, I'm pretty sure he means to shut it up and discharge the many servants, except one or two."

"Oh, what a wicked shame! That glorious place!"

"Yes, Joanne, far too glorious to live in with any comfort, according to him, of course—and too magnificent to ever be a home!"

"What perfect nonsense! Any woman who is a woman can make any place a home, and does, of course!"

"Will you, Joanne?"

"Will I what, pray?"

"Somewhere, some time make a home for me?"

"Mr. Anson! Whatever are you saying?"

"Precisely what I mean, Joanne. A home for your handyman who has knocked and been knocked about the world ashore and afloat, and has never known or dreamed, until lately, what a blessing and truly sacred place a home may be. So will you so bless me, Joanne?"

He asked this vital question in his pleasant, ordinary tone of voice and with no mention of that one most essential word, old as the hills, sweet and new as tomorrow's dawn, a word so often misused, misplaced, mistimed and mistaken (alas!) for the real and sacred thing it is and ever should be: Nicholas never once uttered the word "love".

Therefore and wherefore, after they had gone some while in silence, Joanne said in voice passionless as his own had been:

"Mr. Anson, I think—no, I'm sure you are the most forward, audacious, presumptuous man I ever met!"

"Presumptuous, yes!" he replied, caressing her mare's glossy neck with bronzed, powerful hand. "Knowing life as I do, I'm pretty sure all lovers are presumptuous, because no man is really worthy of a truly good woman."

"Which," she retorted, "is mere sentimental rubbish!"

"Well, I am perhaps a sentimental person, or let's say a man of sentiment who has seen so much of evil and brutality that he has become an idealist."

"But why go anywhere near such brutal evil?"

"Circumstances compelled me, Joanne, for I——"

"That," she exclaimed, scornfully, "is the excuse for incapacity, the excuse for weakness! We all blame circumstance for our own faults!"

"Cor love a duck!" exclaimed Nicholas in awed tone. "Minerva on horseback!"

The horse was checked instantly that she might look down on him as the goddess herself might have done, that is to say, with a calm, aloof appraisal.

"No," said she at last, shaking her handsome, stately head, very Minerva-like, "I shall never understand you, nor shall I try!"

"Very well," he answered, as they moved on again, "instead of showing like Minerva, crowned with wisdom and throned in judgment, be your own loveliest self; and since you are such an extremely feminine woman, please tell me how you would set about making a home for the chosen man. Let us suppose I am he, that we are just married——"

"I refuse to suppose anything so impossible—and awful!"

"Mistress mine," he sighed, "the old adage says: 'All things are possible to him who waits!' And I am, or can be, a very patient soul."

"Mr. Anson," she demanded, checking her mare again, "are you intending me to understand this as a proposal of marriage?"

"I am indeed!"

"Then you are indeed the clumsiest, most awkward, unhandiest handyman possible to imagine! And, of course, I refuse utterly, firmly and irrevocably here and now."

"However, Joanne, there is always the future, that mystery wherein dreams and hopes may be realised. If not now—tomorrow, and with each succeeding morrow, I shall hope that you and I may find the blessedness of home, and there uniting——"

Here, with a sound that in anyone else would have been termed "a snort", Joanne urged her mare to a sudden gallop, leaving him to trudge after in the dust of her sudden departure.

CHAPTER XII

Diamond v. *Paste*

IT IS a week later, when Sir Nicholas Harbourne, alighting from his hired cab, pays the smartly top-hatted, box-coated Jehu and, entering the portal of a certain world-famous club, is there greeted by a dignified person, who bows, presents a sealed letter with something of a flourish, and says resoundingly:

"My lord the Earl of Stukely-Deveril awaits you in the card-room, Sir Nicholas."

"The card-room? Thanks!" says Sir Nicholas and, pocketing the letter unopened, makes his way to where my lord the Earl awaits him in one of the very few armchairs permitted in this most fateful of rooms which all too often has been the cause of so many blighted lives and unworthy dying.

The Earl, asprawl in cushioned chair and apparently half asleep as usual, now troubled himself to sit up and greet Sir Nicholas like the old and tried friends they were, enquiring drowsily and with few words as possible:

"'Lo, Nick, how do! Got y' letter last week; been wonderin' what th' dooce? Why want introduction t' Wolverton? The' flo's not our sort, don't b'long. S' why?"

"For a very special purpose, Stooks. I desire to try a flutter with him." The Earl actually sat up, opening those seemingly sleepy though very keen eyes of his.

"Y' mean—cards?"

"Of course."

"N' listen to me, Nick! Y' know his reputation, told y' m'self, but 'll repeat. Flo's most desp'rate gambler in the club, plays dev'lish high and too dev'lish lucky— ruined several already, poor devils! Consequently he's becoming suspect—sharping and what not, though can't abs'lootly sure, o' course——"

"And, my dear old Stook, that's why!"

"What's why?"

"Why I mean to prove him, play him and make sure."

"Nick, y' are askin' f' trouble."

"But may save trouble for others; besides, as I say, I have another and most particular purpose. So play him I will."

"He'll fleece y' Nick, bound to!"

"I'll chance that, old fellow."

"Always stubborn as dooced mule, Nick—have it y' own way, as usual! H'ever I s'pose y' can 'ford to drop a thousand or so now. Which 'minds me—what been doin' in th' country all this time, Nick?"

"Learning farm work."

"Ha—ver' good! England's real prosperity is in th' land, not these damn mills 'n' factories 'n' so on; always was 'n' will be! Going to live there—Grayladies? Hey?"

"I'm not sure, Stooks. It all depends."

"Not on oof, y'r damn rich nowadays, Nick—so what?"

"Circumstance, old fellow, just one."

"Ha! Any good 'quiring name o' this 'Circumstance', Nick?"

"Not a bit, old boy."

"Hope y' not thinkin' o' committin' matrimony, m' poor fool, eh?"

"Stooks, there's nothing I desire more."

"Then all I can say is—ha, there's y' man!"

All this time the great room had been filling—a cheerful and numerous company; but as the chairs at the many tables became occupied, this laughter and merry clamour subsided, while waiters sped silently to and fro in answer to lifted finger or eyebrow while new packs of cards were being opened; and it was upon this growing and ever more pregnant hush that an imperious voice now broke, saying:

"Waiter, I ordered and want my usual corner table!"

"And it has been reserved for your lordship."

"Jeakins," said the Earl, beckoning the nearest waiter, "desire Lord Wolverton t' step this way, compliments, o' course."

Lord Wolverton's approach was leisurely, his bow of ironic ceremoniousness as he said rather grimly:

"This is indeed a surprise, my lord!"

"Glad you 'preciate it, sir. H'ever, m' old friend here, Sir Nicholas Harbourne, desires game with you. Nick, Lord Wolverton—can y' 'blige m' friend, m' lord?"

"With greatest pleasure, sir. We shall now be five, an ideal number for poker!"

"Poker?" enquired Sir Nicholas.

"Yes, sir; I seldom play anything else—this most engaging American game, a finer development of our old

English game of 'Brag', they tell me. You must have heard of it?"

"Certainly, my lord, and years ago I even tried my hand at it."

"Excellent! Then you shall try your hand at it again since you so desire and—if agreeable to my three friends— ah, yonder they come, I'll go and enquire—pardon me."

"B'ware, Nick, b'ware!" murmured the Earl. "Hawks, damn hawks 'n' carrion kites—pluck y'r every dooced feather, m' poor, damn pigeon!"

"Well, let 'em, Stooks, if they can, but——"

"Ha, Nick, besides you they've 'nother poor, damn pigeon, very young and dooced fluffy, young Hardy—just down from 'varsity, young fool! Sleepin' here tonight, Nick?"

"Yes."

"So 'm I, and I'll go do it now—don't want t' see the damn feathers fly. Goo' night!"

"Good night, old fellow. Wolverton's beckoning, so wish me luck."

"I do, but 't won't avail, y'll be stripped bare as a damn coot afore dawn!"

Then Sir Nicholas, crossing to Lord Wolverton's table, bowed to his three friends, namely Sir Toby Tofton, an excessively languid gentleman of indeterminate age, Colonel Donovan, military and slightly grim, and Mr. Hardy, nervously young.

Lord Wolverton, taking up one of the many unopened packs of cards at his elbow, broke the seal, threw out the joker and ran the cards through his large though very nimble fingers, saying:

"Since the game may be somewhat novel to—ah—some of us, I propose we begin very moderately, gentlemen, let us say a ten-shilling ante and a pound to play."

"As you will!" murmured Sir Toby.

"Agreed!" quoth the Colonel.

"Y-Yes!" said young Mr. Hardy, gulping.

"Ah, no!" sighed Sir Nicholas. "I fear this is too steep for me, at least—to begin with. I suggest half a crown ante and five shillings to play. Agreed?"

"Yes, sir!" sighed Mr. Hardy gratefully.

"Haw, chicken-feed!" exclaimed the Colonel.

"My dear Harbourne," smiled Lord Wolverton, "I fear this would be merest waste of time. But since you are, I believe, but slightly acquainted with the game, we will, for your sake, at least for the present, remit the stakes to five shillings, calling ten, with a betting limit of twenty pounds—eh, Sir Nicholas?"

"No, my lord, my betting limit must be ten pounds for a while at least."

Lord Wolverton, still fondling the cards, showed his teeth in a smile so very like a sneer that Sir Nicholas turned to gaze at these teeth until their somewhat heavy lips hid them, as my lord replied:

"I commend your caution, sir; ten pounds it shall be. Now as regards these very many bone or ivory discs, these counters or chips, m' dear Harbourne, the blue we value at a pound, the red at ten shillings and the white at five. How many do you buy, Harbourne?"

"Oh, well," he replied, hesitantly, "I'll take twenty pounds' worth."

"So few?" said my lord, counting out the required

number. "I fear you will be buying again soon, m' dear Harbourne."

"Very well, my lord, when I must, I will."

"What of you, Toby?"

"Gimme two hundred pounds' worth as a starter."

"There you are, Toby, pray count them and make sure. What for you, Mr. Hardy?"

"A—hundred, if you please, my lord."

"And you, Colonel?"

"Four hundred, Wolverton, I'm determined on action tonight."

"Splendid!" said my lord. "To you, m' dear fellow, and may they multiply with action. And now for those not entirely conversant with this American game, I will explain the value of the various hands, naming them in order of precedence thus: one pair; two pairs; three of a kind; a straight, meaning a sequence; a flush, meaning all of one suit; a full-house, meaning three and a pair; fours; a straight flush, meaning a sequence in the same suit; a royal straight flush, meaning ace to the ten of the same suit. And now I think we may begin."

The deal falling to Sir Toby, he distributed the cards with a nice dexterity; the hands were taken up, studied and certain of them thrown aside.

"One, please!" said Mr. Hardy.

"Three!" the Colonel demanded truculently.

"Two for me!" said Sir Toby.

"And the same here!" said Sir Nicholas.

"I now bet ten pounds!" said Mr. Hardy.

"There's your ten. Demme, I must see you, sir," said the Colonel.

"Sir, I must call your bet also!" said my lord, covering the bets.

"Out!" sighed Sir Nicholas, tossing his hand into the discard.

"I'll see you also, b'gad," drawled Sir Toby.

"Gentlemen," said young Hardy, almost apologetically, "I have a straight——"

"Beats me!" growled the Colonel.

"Me also!" nodded his lordship.

"Take th' money!" said Sir Toby.

"Which, my dear Hardy, would have been so much more," sighed his lordship, "so very much more but for our friend Harbourne's somewhat excessive caution."

Now at this suggestion young Mr. Hardy, flushed with success as he collected his winnings, glanced askance on Sir Nicholas, and frowned, saying, and quite boldly now:

"My lord, I am perfectly willing—indeed I should enjoy playing for higher stakes."

"Hear, hear!" growled the Colonel.

"Bravo!" chirruped Sir Toby.

"So it seems," smiled Lord Wolverton, "we four are agreed. How say you now, Harbourne?"

"Well," he replied, "I'm beginning to remember something of the game; besides, it appears fairly simple, so—have with you, sirs."

"Excellent!" exclaimed my lord, clapping those large, smooth hands of his softly. "Then from now on we'll make the ante five pounds, ten to play and the betting limit a hundred pounds. Gentlemen, how say you?"

"Good enough!" murmured Sir Toby.

"Pretty damn steep!" quoth the Colonel.

"Y-Yes!" said young Hardy, gulping again, his boldness quite gone.

"And you, m' dear Sir Nicholas?"

"Anything you like!" he answered lightly. And now, as the Colonel dealt, all leaned nearer the table, watching the fall of each card with new and rather dreadful intensity.

But the next two hands afforded so little of what the Colonel had called "action" that Sir Nicholas began to yawn and, finding his cards worthless, leaned, elbow on table and head in hand, as though becoming drowsy; he was still sitting thus when my lord took up the cards to deal, saying:

"Gentlemen, I hold the buck; this marker which I now put in the kitty making this a jack-pot, which can be opened only by a pair of knaves or better."

Sir Nicholas stirred not, but his eyes were anything but drowsy as, between slightly parted fingers, he watched Lord Wolverton shuffle the cards with those large though extremely nimble fingers of his, and as Sir Nicholas watched thus the motion of each individual finger, his sensitive mouth twitched, this and no more.

With hand not quite steady, young Hardy cut; with hands swiftly dexterous my lord dealt, and, taking up his cards, Sir Nicholas saw three aces and a pair of fours, and, remembering those same large, very nimble fingers, he pushed one blue chip into the kitty, saying:

"I open for one pound!"

"Eh?" exclaimed Sir Toby. "Only one? This lets us all in—ha, something doing; sly, dem sly!"

"And I," said young Hardy stridently, "I raise that to the limit—I bet one hundred pounds!"

"Do ye, b'gad!" exclaimed the Colonel, scowling. "Well, that floors me. I pass out! Up to you, Wolverton."

"Then," said he, smiling, "to get a little action into our very modest game, I will risk—let me see, yes—your hundred, Hardy, and I raise you a hundred up, and await our friend Harbourne."

"Out!" said he, and, tossing away this very powerful hand, saw Lord Wolverton's eyes flicker, wherefore, being now quite sure, his sensitive lips twitched again while the betting progressed precisely as he expected, for :

"I'm away!" sighed Sir Toby.

"And I," said young Hardy, fumbling chips excitedly, "I bet your hundred, my lord, and raise you a hundred more."

"Ha, action at last!" quoth the Colonel. "What d'you say to that, Wolverton—bet's with you!"

"B'Jove, I must think!" said my lord, studying his hand rather anxiously. "None of us drew cards, pat hands all; this is phenomenal! Hardy must be devilish strong, yet sweet Lady Luck bids me be bold and dare you again. So, my dear Hardy, here is your hundred with a hundred of mine."

At this, young Hardy sank back in his chair to gaze at his cards with quite fearful anxiety, then enquired rather breathlessly :

"How much is there in the kitty?"

"About five hundred pounds."

"Then, my lord, I—I must see, I must know what you have."

"Which will cost you another hundred, m' dear fellow."

"Yes, yes, of course!" said eager, trembling Youth, pushing the last of his chips into the kitty. "There's my hundred; pray show your hand. I hold a full-house, three kings and a pair of queens."

"Alas, m' dear Hardy, I show you four threes, small in themselves but together sufficiently potent!" said my lord, gathering his winnings with hands whose clutch seemed unpleasantly avid, or so thought Sir Nicholas.

"Oh!" gasped Youth. "Yes, I see. Well, I—I must buy more counters. Another hundred pounds' worth, please."

The game progressed with varying success, except for young Hardy, who so consistently over-valued his cards that, as the clocks chimed, this midnight hour found him crouched at a writing table in remote corner, scrawling his third I.O.U., found Lord Wolverton vastly the winner and therefore jubilant, the Colonel fairly so, yet grim as ever, Sir Toby about even and yawning, with Sir Nicholas some fifty pounds out.

This same hour also seemed a signal for the ending or temporary cessation of play, for once again was sound of talk and laughter as many of the players rose to depart, and with them young Hardy, who, with smile that made his youthful face ghastly, gave his I.O.U. to Lord Wolverton, saying:

"Good night, my lord! Gentlemen, I—I thank you for —the game." Having said which, Youth, pale as a young ghost, like a ghost was gone, unheeded by any except Sir Nicholas.

"Well, I've had about enough!" said the Colonel, pocketing his winnings.

"Same here!" yawned Sir Toby. 'And, demme, Wolverton, but you're lucky as usual!"

"Yes!" he laughed. "Sweet Lady Luck is usually gracious enough to smile upon her humble devotee. Good night and farewell till our next merry meeting. Well, Harbourne, are you off, too?"

"No, I'm sleeping here."

"Aha! Then how about playing on, just you and I, something with more devil in it, eh?"

"But isn't poker a poor game for two?"

"It is, my dear fellow. I was meaning a variation of poker, called 'stud'. You've heard of it?"

"I fancy so, but I should like you to explain it."

"Oh, certainly! It's a perfectly simple game. We play five cards, one hidden face down, the other four shown face up, and we bet on each card. The hidden card is the power, the threat of the unknown which governs the betting and by which the bluffing is done—if the stakes are high enough! It's a speedy and, as I say, perfectly simple game, as you'll see—if you are game."

"I will so endeavour, my lord!" said Sir Nicholas and, taking a new pack of cards, he broke the seal, dropped the joker, then he shuffled.

"Lowest deals!" said my lord, cutting.

"And yours it is!" said Sir Nicholas, having dealt a card each, and passed the pack. Now this time, quite openly and with very evident keenness, he watched those big dexterous fingers as they shuffled and reshuffled ere they placed the two cards face down, which done:

"Now," said my lord, "before we look at our hidden pasteboards, seeing the hour is somewhat late and that we are only two and both game, I propose we make the sky our limit."

"Meaning, of course, no limit, my lord?"

"Precisely! Only so can one bluff with any hope of success. Well, Harbourne, are you truly game?"

Sir Nicholas glanced somewhat anxiously from Lord Wolverton's vast array of chips, coins, notes and I.O.U.s to his own slender, very modest stack and hesitated so long that my lord, becoming impatient, ventured a sneer:

"You are a somewhat over-cautious player, Harbourne!"

"Your lordship is perfectly right. I am! But if you desire such ferocious, cut-throat play, so be it."

"Bravo, m' dear fellow! Now we peep at our buried cards and bet accordingly."

"Ten pounds, my lord!"

"And ten up, Harbourne! Are you content?"

"Perfectly!" replied Sir Nicholas, his eyes still intent.

"Then I deal again, giving you—an ace, b'gad, and to myself—the queen of spades, and ace bets."

"Ten pounds, my lord."

"And twenty more. Do you venture a raise?"

"Certainly not."

"Then I deal our second shown cards—to you the three of diamonds, and to myself—the ten of hearts. And ace still bets."

"Ten pounds, my lord."

"You become slightly monotonous, Harbourne! Your ten and fifty more. Does that hold you?"

"Hard and fast!" said Sir Nicholas, adding the fifty.

"I now deal our third cards, to you the—nine of hearts, and to myself the—six of spades. And ace still bets."

"Ten pounds, my lord."

"Your ten and a hundred."

"Your hundred and five more."

"Five pounds, Harbourne?"

"Hundreds, my lord."

"Eh, what—five hundred? Ah well, with unlimited betting and plenty of nerve, bluffing is easy! I cover your five hundred, and now deal our fourth and last cards—to you the knave of spades and to myself the—five of hearts. And ace bets still."

"A thousand!" said Sir Nicholas.

"So! A thousand pounds, d'ye say?" My lord frowned at all the shown cards, peered at his hidden one.

"Harbourne," said he between smiling lips but with a glare in his eyes, "you shall not steal such a pretty sum from me on a bluff. I call it and damn hard! There's my thousand to see if you can better my queens, now turn your card."

Sir Nicholas did so and showed another ace. Lord Wolverton dashed the pack down so violently that many of the cards fell to the floor, whereat was a stir and mutter of disapproval, and, glancing up, he saw they were ringed by a crowd of spectators, for news had sped that in this historic room, where great fortunes and vast estates had been lost and won, another such desperate game was in progress, wherefore, late though the hour, this hushed, soft-footed company had gathered to watch the fall of these cards that were, it seemed, to be the ruin of yet

G

another blind devotee of that most fickle goddess, "Chance". Nor were dramatic incidents lacking in this game; indeed they happened so often and rapidly as to keep the hushed spectators on the very tiptoe of excitement —this quite merciless game of limitless betting that with each hand, with each individual card, became ever more desperate and grim as great sums of money were lost, won and lost again. One such dramatic moment occurred when Sir Nicholas, dealing, gave his opponent a king of spades and himself the queen of hearts. My lord, somewhat flushed, cried:

"Five hundred on my king!"

"And a thousand more!" said Sir Nicholas.

"Which I call! There's my thousand!" Whereat Sir Nicholas, laughing ruefully, swept his cards together, saying:

"Take the money!"

"Ha, bluffing again, hey?" demanded my lord, with fierce laugh. "Caught ye that time, did I, hey?"

"You did indeed!" sighed Sir Nicholas. "But I like bluffing. I find it quite pleasant to win with nothing against a fairly good hand, as I have done once or twice. Yes, I enjoy bluffing."

"Do ye, b'gad! Well, you've just bluffed yourself out of three thousand pounds! So don't try it too often."

"Oh, but I shall. I fancy bluffing is my game—and I hope your lordship finds me game enough."

His lordship actually snarled.

And now they played as no men should, with bitter animosity on my lord's side countered by an infuriating ironic courtesy. So this battle of cards, nerves and money raged until came the final devastating play, when Sir Nicholas, dealing, enquired:

"Pray, my noble lord, how much on your hidden card?"

"Ten pounds!"

"I must beg you, gracious sir, to make it twenty—so! Now, my lord, copying your own admired manner, I deal to you—the king of diamonds and to myself the—knave of hearts. And king bets——"

"I know it, sir, I know it! Fifty pounds on my king!"

"Your fifty, gentle sir, and two hundred more on my knave."

"Your two hundred, Harbourne, with five hundred up on my king. Does that satisfy you—ha?"

"So little, my dear lord, that you must pay yet another five hundred or retire and——"

"Retire be damned!" exclaimed my lord, as, with furious gesture, he added the further sum, which done, Sir Nicholas dealt again, saying in smiling mockery of his scowling opponent:

"I now proceed to deal our second cards, giving to you, my gracious lord—another king, b'Jove, and to myself the—nine of hearts. And your pair of kings bet——"

"Five—hundred—pounds!" cried my lord, fiercely jubilant.

"To which, my lord, you must add another thousand."

"Ha, with pleasure—there it is!"

"Good, my good lord! I now deal our third cards—bestowing on your noble self the—two of diamonds and on myself the—eight of hearts. And your pair of kings bet——"

"Five—hundred—pounds!"

"Whereto I must trouble your lordship to add yet another thousand."

"There it is! Deal the next card, man—deal, I say, deal."

"Patience, good my lord, patience! For this, being our fourth and last shown card, is therefore most fateful and may prove fatal to one of us——"

"Deal, damn you, deal!"

"My poor lord, does suspense so harrow your soul, so rack your nerves that you forget to comport yourself as a gentleman and member of this club? Oh, fie! However, to end your mental stress I now proceed to deal our fourth and all-deciding cards—first reminding you that here in the pool—or should I say kitty?—we have the pleasing sum of six thousand three hundred odd——"

"I know it! Damme, I have eyes! Deal and be done!"

"Done it is, most gentle of lords, and 'done' indeed one of us will be most certainly! Now then, I proceed to deal our fourth and all-deciding cards, to you the—now kind Dame Fortune help me—a third king and to my humbled, anxious self the—ten of hearts. And your three kings have first——"

"Five thousand pounds, Harbourne."

"Ten thousand up, Wolverton!"

Dumbstruck, my lord glared, lolling back in his chair; Sir Nicholas smiled; while among the onlookers was a sudden stir, a gasping inhalation, an excited whispering hushed to watchful expectancy as my lord demanded hoarsely:

"Harbourne, say that again!"

"Fifteen thousand up, Wolverton!"

"No, your bet was ten."

"It was, but is now fifteen, and will be twenty unless——"

"Damnation, sir, I refuse to be rushed! Your bet was ten thousand and such it must and shall remain!"

"Very well," sighed Sir Nicholas, taking out his watch and placing it upon the table, "at ten thousand it shall remain for five minutes, at the end of which time my bet will rise to twenty."

My lord glared from his smiling opponent to that sequence in hearts, enumerating them aloud as they lay, thus:

"Jack, nine, eight, ten!"

"A fairly good bluffing hand, my lord!" murmured Sir Nicholas suggestively, "being a possible straight, a more improbable flush, a more unlikely and most improbable straight flush or—nothing at all. A hand of power or merest futility. The harassing question for you to decide is which, and to bet accord——"

"Dammit, Harbourne, be silent and let me think!"

"And your lordship has still four minutes!"

Lord Wolverton's flushed face showed moist; he wiped at it furiously with his handkerchief, his scowling gaze always upon that sequence of hearts.

"Harbourne," said he at last, still wiping at face and neck, "yours is such a perfect bluffing hand that, knowing your play, I wonder at my hesitation——"

"So do I, my lord."

"Very well, then, to make speedy end, I cover your ten thousand and raise you another—hundred pounds."

"Where to, right valorous lord, I add now fifteen thousand!"

Again all about these desperate gamblers was vague stir, then a hushed stillness so profound that all might hear my lord's heavy breathing and the drumming of his nervous fingers on the table; and when at last he spoke, it was in harsh, broken gasps very unlike his usual smooth tones:

"No—no, by God—I refuse to be bluffed—you shan't steal from me again—no—not this time, damn you! I cover your bet—you shall have my I.O.U. for it. Now, turn your card—as I do—and beat my four kings if you can."

"My lord, with pleasure!" replied Sir Nicholas and, flipping his hidden card face up, showed the queen of hearts, saying:

"Yes, here she is, gentle lady, bless her!"

Dumbstruck, Lord Wolverton gazed—then, uttering a strangled cry worse than any groan, sank back in his chair and seemed positively to shrink; and, beholding his agonised distress that he made no effort to hide, the shamed onlookers stole silently away.

CHAPTER XIII

How Lord Wolverton Wrote a Letter, and Why

SO NOW in this great, empty room these two men sat fronting each other speechlessly across the littered table that had been their battle-ground. For some time they remained thus, Lord Wolverton breathing stertorously, while Sir Nicholas, very ostentatiously, counted his enormous gains, until my lord, unable to endure the sight, writhed in his chair and, groaning, spoke at last:

"Harbourne, I—I am ruined!"

"Hush!" said Sir Nicholas. "Pray don't distract me until I have assessed the value of this ill-gotten wealth."

"But, Harbourne—for God's sake listen—I'm an utterly ruined man!"

"There have been others besides yourself, Wolverton, notably poor young Hardy—he proved a far gamer loser than your groaning lordship!"

"Oh, damn and curse you!" cried my lord in sudden paroxysm of fury. "You and only you are the devilish cause of it all! You, Harbourne, you alone have ruined me utterly—utterly!"

"Of course!" answered Sir Nicholas, glancing up. "That is why I troubled to play you!" Then he went on with his counting while my lord stared at him now in amazed and angry bewilderment.

"Then you—you meant to ruin me?"

"Certainly!"

"But why, Harbourne, and how—how in the devil's name could you be sure?"

"My lord," replied Sir Nicholas wearily, "I played with the purpose of ruining you for a very good and lovely purpose, and found you a very indifferent player and quite second-rate card-sharper, for——"

"Eh? What—what? Are you—dare you suggest——"

"Don't bluster, Wolverton; we both know you are a cheat. I saw you at it sev——"

My lord leapt from his chair, but a long arm powerfully out-thrust hurled him back again, and Sir Nicholas continued: "I saw you at it five several times. After that I didn't bother to watch but played accordingly. You are fairly quick, but those large fingers of yours need a deal more schooling——"

Here my lord made another attempt to leap at his tormentor, with the same result.

"Sit still!" said Sir Nicholas. "Don't be such a fool of a lord, my lord! Sit tight and listen to me——"

"Harbourne," he cried, "all night I've wondered why, every now and then, your face, your air, seemed so dev'lish unpleasantly familiar! I suppose I must have seen you somewhere or other, and not so long ago; the question is—where?"

"Oh, probably here or there, Wolverton—mine is such a common, or garden, face you may have seen it anywhere or everywhere! However, you were informing me how very completely I have ruined you. Pray go on."

"Damme, what more can I say than that you—you have ruined me?"

"Not beyond redemption, I hope?"

Thus reminded, Lord Wolverton, forgetting everything except self-pity, bowed his head between clasped hands and answered brokenly:

"Yes—yes, you have indeed—ruined me—beyond all hope of redemption! You have my all—houses—land—livestock—by God, I haven't even a roof to shelter me! You have—everything!"

"Not quite, my lord. You still hold Edward Marsden's I.O.U. for twelve thousand odd pounds."

"Well, what of it? And how the devil do you know?"

"No matter! Is it get-at-able?"

"Yes. Why?"

"Because I want it, my lord! And I want it tonight! So I suggest you go and fetch it."

"As it happens, I have it on me."

"Very well, show it to me."

"Why?"

"I'll tell you when I've seen it."

"What the devil business is it of yours?"

"Show me and learn."

Slowly and sullenly my lord drew from some inner pocket an ornate letter-case, whence he extracted a folded paper, saying:

"Keep your distance, Harbourne."

"Fool, let me read it!"

"You may do so from where you are—and keep your hands on the table. Though why should I let you read it?"

"For your own good, perhaps."

"Aha, so—that's it! Well now, Harbourne, if you want to buy this and play beneficent Providence to the folk at Fallowdene, meaning, of course, that armful of warm loveliness——"

"Show it or be damned!"

"So that is your purpose, hey? Good! Now—if I sell —it shall be at my own figure! Take a look, then—and stay where you are!" As he spoke, and, keeping well out of reach, my lord unfolded the paper and Sir Nicholas read this:

"Jan. 1. 18–. This to certify that I owe Charles, Lord Wolverton, Twelve Thousand Three Hundred pounds.
EDWARD MARSDEN."

Having scanned this very carefully, Sir Nicholas nodded, saying:

"Yes, it seems genuine——"

"Genuine? Of course it is! What d'ye mean?"

"Having regard to your poker-play I was naturally a trifle dubious."

"Well, now, Harbourne, are you prepared to redeem it —at my price?"

"No, at mine! I'll buy the damned thing for three times its stated value."

"Three times? Eh? D'ye mean it? Three times? This would be thirty-six thousand nine hundred pounds——"

"Which, thanks to gracious Dame Fortune, I can afford. Well, is it a deal?"

"Yes—yes, of course! Naturally! I—I should be a fool to refuse."

"Undoubtedly!"

"Suppose, considering your stupendous winnings—I should demand more?"

"You would be more of a fool than I deem you! This money. I will pay you so soon as Miss Marsden receives your letter."

"Eh? What letter?"

"The one you are about to write enclosing this very cursed paper, this damned thing by which you might have compelled her to beggary—or marriage with your lordship, which would have been infinitely worse, of course! Now come and write your letter."

Thus, presently seated at that small writing-table where young Hardy had scrawled his admissions of debt with such tremulous fingers, Lord Wolverton now wrote at the dictation of Sir Nicholas:

"—*Club London.*

June 20, 18–.

"DEAR MISS MARSDEN,

"The devil being not so black as he is painted, I take pleasure in returning your father's promissory note, with the hope that it may relieve you of all further worry.

"This from your sincere well-wisher,

"CHARLES, LORD WOLVERTON."

"So?" exclaimed my lord, appending his signature with prodigious flourish. "So it seems you intend I shall play Providence, or appear to. I wonder why? What's your game, Harbourne?"

"One your lordship couldn't understand. So address this envelope instead."

Scowling in futile anger, my lord obeyed, and, watched closely by Sir Nicholas, folded letter and enclosure together and thrust them into the envelope, then, smiting the table with passionate fist, demanded:

"Now what, dammit, what security do you offer me for——"

"Be hushed, sweet lord, and oblige me with pen, paper."

Taking these, Sir Nicholas scribbled forthwith:

"I promise to pay, on demand, the sum of thirty-six thousand nine hundred pounds to Lord Wolverton for value received.

"NICHOLAS ANTHONY HARBOURNE."

"There you are, Wolverton! Take it and give me your letter!" The exchange made, Sir Nicholas thrust this letter into his breast pocket, saying:

"Now, my lord, I am happy to bid you good night, or, better still, goodbye."

"Harbourne, before we part, will you—may I know the amount of your winnings?"

"Well, roughly, right noble lord, with the money you stole from your friends and the sum I stole from you, it is about——"

"Eh—what? Stole, d'ye say? What the devil—you—you stole—from me?"

"Certainly! You cheated your friends quite frequently. I cheated you merely once, but—effectively!"

"Ha—that last deal!"

"Precisely!"

"You—you set those last hands!"

"Well, of course! And, of course, exceedingly well! My fingers have not lost their cunning. You see, I learned the craft in a harder school than you, where a mistake meant knife or bullet, like as not——"

"So you cheated me and dare confess it, do you?"

"No, you fool, I announce the fact with great pleasure!"

"Then by heaven I'll denounce you! I'll proclaim your infamy! I'll have you expelled this club for the thief and sharping trickster you are! I say I'll——"

"So ho!" laughed Sir Nicholas. "My lord Pot will call Sir Kettle black! Extremely comical, Wolverton! The more so because my lord Pot is already suspected as being infernally sooty! So, my lord Fool, do and say of me as you will, your own disrepute is such that no one will believe you. Try, most futile lord, and see."

"Harbourne, if ever I can get even with you I will!"

"Wolverton, I don't doubt it! Meanwhile I leave you to think out ways and means—if you can think."

Then Sir Nicholas nodded and went blithely up to bed. But before undressing he drew out Lord Wolverton's letter and with it that other he had received upon entering the club, and this directed to him in an unknown hand; so he opened it and read this:

"To Sir Nicholas Harbourne.

"Honoured sir, we the undersigned in the name of every grateful tenant on your estate of Harbourne, beg to express to the best of our ability our deeply sincere and united gratitude for your gracious, most unexpected and well-nigh unbelievable magnanimity in the matter of our rentals. Sir, you have thus freed us from great tribulation, relieving us of care and constant anxiety. Sir, not a man or woman of us all but prays the Almighty to bless you in this life and the life hereafter. Sir, we can say no more except that henceforth, being happy, we shall one and all work with better heart and to better purpose.

"Signed in all gratitude,

JOHN MARTIN,
ELIHU DENT,
THOMAS BAILY,
JOS. BOWYER,
JOANNE MARSDEN."

"Now God bless her!" said Nicholas, touching this last signature with his lips. And it was with this letter beneath his pillow, therefore, that he went to bed and presently to the blessedness of dreamless slumber.

CHAPTER XIV

How a Letter was Burnt and Priscilla's Woe Turned to Joy

"SO IT seems, Aunt," said Joanne, glancing up from the letter she had just been reading aloud, "it is perfectly evident that we, and especially you, have dreadfully and cruelly misjudged poor Charles! This proves him to be a truly noble lord!"

"A noble fiddlestick, my dear sweet fool!" said Aunt Jemima, above her busy knitting-pins. "The man never did an unselfish act in his life."

"Aunt, how can you be so harsh?"

"Easily, Joanne! Do tigers and leopards ever change their spots and things? No, certainly not! Neither can Lord Wolverton. He was very spotty as a boy, I remember. Consequently only a fool would think he can."

"Aunt, do you call me a fool because at last I begin to appreciate Charles at his true worth?"

"I did and I do, my dear! Your folly impels me——"

"But good gracious—here before your very eyes is proof of his unselfishness! He has returned this hateful I.O.U. without my asking; he has given it to me because he saw my—my agonised distress. Isn't this a splendidly generous, truly noble act?"

"My dear," said Aunt Jemima in her serene and gentle way, "you now compel me to say you are not merely a fool but a most complete one."

"Then you are very unkind to me and quite wickedly unjust to poor Charles! Do you deny him every virtue?"

"Yes, most of them! I remember him also as a nasty, plump, selfishly-greedy boy and he has grown into a plumply selfish, greedy man."

"He is considered a very handsome man, Aunt, and at the hunt and assembly balls he can pick and choose his partners; he's a beautiful dancer!"

"And what beside, my dear?"

"He is a really splendid figure on horseback!"

"Has he asked you to marry him lately?"

"Of course! He's always doing so, and I could scarcely do better—in a way."

"You could not do worse in every way, my dear!"

"Goodness me, Aunt, I never heard you speak of poor Charles so bitterly! You sound quite vindictive —and just after he has been so very kind and generous, too!"

"He could never be either, Joanne!"

"But he is! He must be! Here is the absolute proof! By returning this hateful thing, unasked and of his own free will, Charles has endeared himself to me far more than I ever thought possible!"

"But I don't believe it was!"

"Was what, Aunt?"

"Returned of his own free will."

"Then what in the world do you believe?"

"That he was compelled."

"Oh? Who by? Whoever could compel Charles to do anything against his will? Tell me who, pray?"

"Circumstance!"

"What circumstance? Aunt, whatever do you mean?"

"Precisely what I say."

"Well, Aunt, I haven't the vaguest idea——"

"Oh, but you have, child—every now and then you have the most astounding ideas—mostly wrong, of course —like your foolish idea of Wolverton's generosity! Which reminds me—has our handyman returned yet?"

"No—at least I haven't seen him."

"Then I wish he would for all our sakes, and especially Priscilla's; she grieves for him quite dreadfully!"

"Yes," sighed Joanne, "and every night prays for his return. He seems to have bewitched the poor little soul— yes, and you, too, Aunt!"

"Perhaps, my dear; however, I like him and miss him far more than I thought possible. He has been gone over a week now."

"Eight days!" said Joanne, then, flushing hotly, frowned at herself, glanced askance at Aunt Jemima, which serenely wise lady was apparently counting the stitches of the small stocking she was engaged upon, who sighed:

"And my little Priscilla calling for him every evening so soon as she's back from school, faithful little soul! Business of his own may have taken him away, unless you have flown into one of your tempers and sent him off at a moment's notice. Have you?"

"No, Aunt, I have—not! And am I so passionate?"

"Extremely tempestuous, my dear, furiously sudden

H

and as suddenly calm. But I suppose this is to be expected by reason of your——"

"My hateful red hair——"

"Auburn, my dear."

"Anyhow, I hate it now as I did at school when they called me 'carrots'!"

"It has become much darker since then, my dear, quite becomingly so."

"Well, I hate and detest it!"

"However, there are some who seem to admire it, especially—one!"

"Oh?" murmured Joanne. "Who, Aunt?"

"Lord Wolverton, of course."

"Oh!" exclaimed Joanne.

"And—one other."

"What other?"

"Our handyman."

"Oh!" said Joanne, murmurous again. "How do you know?"

"He said as much—a quite remarkable remark."

"What, Aunt, pray?"

"That in your hair was a flame to guide a man through life."

"Oh!" said Joanne for the fourth time and softer than ever; and then: "Which was ridiculously high-flown and perfectly absurd, and impertinently presumptuous, too! The man's assurance is quite—overwhelming!"

"Yes, he is indeed so calmly sure and positive that I find him a very restful person. Has he asked you to marry him?"

"Yes."

"And you refused him! May I know why?"

"Because I have no wish to be married. Besides, he didn't ask properly! And besides again," said she, glancing askance at Aunt Jemima, "there's dear, kind and nobly generous Charles!" At this Aunt Jemima actually and positively snorted; wherefore Joanne, sly-smiling, took up my lord's letter to sigh over it, saying very tenderly:

"It is our dear, our generous Charles we have to thank for ridding us of the incubus, freeing us of this curse——"

"Meaning, your poor father's promissory note, my dear?"

"Yes, Aunt, here it is—at last, thanks to Charles, and——"

"Are you sure that is the actual paper my unhappy brother wrote, his genuine signature? Are you quite certain, Joanne?"

"Yes, though it looks as if his poor hand had faltered in places, and here is a great blot just below his name."

"And no wonder, my dear, it was written in great distress of mind and was, I believe, the ultimate cause of his death! Let me look at it." So Joanne gave this same fateful paper to Aunt Jemima, who glanced at it, nodded, sighed and placed it, with deliberate care, precisely where the great, smouldering logs on the hearth glowed brightest; so was a brief flame, a wisp of smoke and that most troublous paper was not.

"Aunt!" cried Joanne, leaping afoot. "Oh what have you done?"

"Freed us all from a killing burden we should never have borne. Now sit down and thank God for blessing you with a common-sense aunt! But what now?" she enquired as in at them through the open casement came Bill's tousled head to shake itself at them very ominously.

"Oh, Miss Jo!" he sighed. "Ah, Mistus Jemima marm, it do break me 'eart for to see that child, our Miss Prissy, come arunning so eager-like, calling 'Anthony', and him not showing; she questions me and Jarge and Old Joe, together and one arter 'tother: 'Is my Anthony come back to me yet?' And when us has for to tell 'er 'no'—them pretty eyes o' hern fills wi' tears—woeful! But she don't cry, only 'er says, says she, valiant-like, ''e'll come back someday, 'cause I've axed God for him every night, so I'll watch for 'im,' says she. And theer 'er be now, awatchin' the road, same like she've done ever since 'e went."

"Yes," sighed Joanne, "I know how she misses him, Bill, and prays every night for his return, bless her!"

"Ar, but woeful it be, I says, and so do say Jarge and old Joe! If Mist' Anthony don't never come back no more —our liddle Priscilla'll vade and pine 'erself into 'er liddle grave, ar—no question! So me and Jarge and Joe be so bold to ax ee, Miss Jo, if so be as you've turned 'im away —if ee can't turn 'im on again——"

"But I haven't turned him away, Bill. Good gracious, no! Mr. Anson went of his own accord, and I'm wondering——" Borne to them on the stilly evening air came a shrill, glad cry:

"An—toe—nee! Oh, my Anthony!"

"Lord!" exclaimed Bill. "Lord love us arl, 'e's come back 'ome!" And, uttering the word, away he strode.

Thus presently back indeed came Nicholas, his hob-nailed boots clattering, and upon his shoulder a child whose eyes were radiant with a great gladness.

"Look!" she cried. "Oh, Auntie Jo—look! God's answered my prayers and sent my Anthony back to me just like you said He would if I b'lieved. So here's my Anthony again and so I've brought him home to tea. But, oh, isn't God kind and everything so lovely again."

CHAPTER XV

In which Aunt Jemima Wonders

THE TEA-THINGS had been removed, Priscilla's home-work happily done (with her Anthony's help), and now, having kissed them all "good night", she (unwillingly) was on her way to bed, pausing to say pleadingly:

"But, oh, Anthony, you won't ever, ever leave me again without saying goodbye and when you'll come back to me again, will you?"

"Never, sweetheart!" he replied fervently.

"Well now, I'll take me to bed, Auntie Jo, if you'll go 'long with me and hear me say my prayers and tuck me up, like all nice good aunties should."

"Dear, don't I—always?"

"And that's why you're a nice good auntie!"

"Come then, sweetheart——"

"Ooh!" exclaimed Priscilla, as they took hands. "You called me 'sweetheart' like my——"

"So I did! It must be catching. Come along." So, with a last lingering look, Priscilla allowed herself to be led away.

"How perfectly adorable she is!" said Nicholas.

"Which?" demanded Aunt Jemima.

"Both!" he answered, laughing.

"Very well, sit down and talk to your devoted aunt."

"Gladly!" said he, seating himself near the open lattice between fire-glow and twilight. "I love the gloaming, Aunt, but how can you see to knit? And do you always have a fire in summer?"

"My dear nephew, I can knit in the dark, and I have a fire as often as possible, because it is such good company, and sometimes—very useful for burning rubbish."

"How are all things with you here, Aunt?"

"Ah, my dear, the bright Angel of Happiness has spread his pinions above this old house because the curse has vanished—in smoke! I burnt it, my poor brother's promissory note—in my useful fire, Anthony!"

"Good!" he murmured, "oh most excellent of Aunts!"

"And so I'm wondering how to thank my nephew for ridding us of our burden of care, how to express my deep gratitude to our so extremely handy handyman, my dear."

"To me, Aunt? But why should——"

"Of course, Anthony!"

"Oh, but I say, you know, I——"

"Yes, my dear, I do know! I was and am quite perfectly sure that no one but you could possibly have wrought us this blessing, this glad end to our care and worry that, as I say, has been our curse and constant menace."

"Aunt Jemima, pray how did you guess?"

"Nephew Anthony, knowing you now so well, how could I help but know? The question I am simply yearning to ask is—how you did it. So I beg you'll inform me, like dutiful nephew. How, Anthony, how?"

"Very simply, Aunt—by out-sharping a sharper! It was like old times."

"At cards, of course?"

"Yes, my dear."

"Meaning you tricked the wretch, you cheated him better than he cheated you?"

"I did indeed, Aunt!"

"Oh, joy!" she exclaimed, and let fall her knitting to clap her hands and laugh so heartily that presently Nicholas laughed also.

"And you gained all his money?"

"So much it embarrassed me."

"And, of course, he never found out or even suspected you?"

"Not he, my dear. So, when everything was definitely settled, I told him."

"That you had cheated him? Oh, my gracious! Whatever did he then?"

"Blustered and threatened, all to no purpose, of course."

"So you won for us poor Edward's promissory note by the cards, did you, Anthony?"

"I saw no other way, Aunt."

"There was no other way, my dear nephew! And I will never say another word against the cards, because you have made them the means of our salvation—and, oh, my dear, my dear, how—ever can I thank you?"

"By promising, Aunt, that Joanne shall never know, unless she has guessed, which heaven forbid!"

"She has not, my dear, and she never shall, from me—though she is now all gratitude to the Wolverton wretch and singing his praises! And this makes me wonder why on earth you didn't send it in your own name or give it to her personally."

"Well, but, dear aunt, considering how I won it——"

"You need not have told her."

"She would have questioned me——"

"Well, you could have evaded her questions."

"Not her questions, Aunt, anyone's but hers. And I couldn't bear to deceive her; and had I told her the truth she would never have understood as you do, my blessed wise Aunt Jemima, now could she?"

"No. Joanne's young and in some ways a sweetly precious, blindly honourable fool! Oh yes, she is, for she now believes Wolverton, as she says, 'a truly noble nobleman', and regards him almost as a man splendidly generous as Sir Nicholas—which is only to be expected under the circumstances. By the way, you and Sir Nicholas are acquainted she tells me."

"Yes."

"Do you see much of him and often?"

"Now and then, Aunt."

"Joanne says you were at sea together."

"Yes, we were shipmates."

"And ashore together, also?"

"Well—yes."

"Anthony, I'm wondering!"

"Are you, Aunt?"

"Yes, my dear. I have been wondering quite often lately!"

"Oh? Indeed?"

"Very much indeed, Anthony."

"Really, Aunt?"

"Yes—nephew. Why don't you ask me who and what about?" Ensued a pregnant silence save for the click of Aunt Jemima's busy knitting-pins, until she enquired at last: "Shall I tell you?"

"No, not now, Aunt—she's coming! I hear her step on the stair. And pray do, for mercy's sake, remember your promise."

"Oysters, nephew, are babblers compared with your devoted aunt! So, instead of you and Sir Nicholas, I'll tell you of Priscilla, how she called and watched and prayed for you. Indeed she loves you very dearly, Anthony, deeply and most truly!"

"Who does, Aunt?" enquired Joanne, pausing in the doorway.

"Come in, Joanne, no—go out and order the lamps."

"Who loves so deeply, dearly and most truly, pray?"

"All of us, my dear, Priscilla and I and Anthony and you. Now ask Ann for the lamps."

"No, Aunt, please, let us sit a little while in this lovely dusk. And, oh, Mr. Anson, how glad I am to tell you Lord Wolverton is a perfect darling."

"Is he, by Jingo!"

"No, by his own splendidly noble account! He is indeed a grand gentleman and much nobler than I ever imagined or dared hope. Aunt Jemima will have told you he has returned that I.O.U. thing and of his own free will and great goodness——"

"Dearest Joanne," said Aunt Jemima very abruptly,

"your loving aunt said nothing of the sort or kind, as you must remember!"

"But, Mr. Anson, don't you argee with me——"

"Yes, with all my heart, mistress mine!"

"That Lord Wolverton's conduct is truly noble and generous?" And between shut teeth Nicholas answered:

"S-s-sertainly——"

"Not!" added Aunt Jemima.

"So tomorrow," said Joanne, seating herself by the open lattice, "I shall ride over to the manor and try to thank him and probably bring him back to tea."

"Ha!" murmured Aunt Jemima. "Then Priscilla and I and probably my nephew will take ours in the fresh air, the rick-yard or home meadow."

"How sweetly thoughtful of you, dearest Aunt, for Charles and I shall have so much to say to each other, alone—concerning—the future."

"So shall we, my sweet pet, concerning the past, Anthony and I."

"May I know who's past, Aunt dearest?"

"The past of all concerned, my love! Yours and Anthony's and——"

In at them through the open window came Bill's head to say:

"Ax-cuse—me, ladies! But they pigsties, Mist' Anthony, eh?"

"Pigsties, precisely!" said Nicholas. "Pigs pays, Mistus Jo, so pigs there must be, eh, Bill, pigs and yet more pigs?"

"Ar, no question, sir! And I got ee that theer load o'

bricks wi' timber as should do right praper—will I show ee afore I goes 'ome, sir?"

"Bill, I'll with thee! Good night, dear Aunt Jemima! Mistress mine, adieu until——"

"Mr. Anson, I am—not—your—— Oh, it is an abominable phrase!"

"Not so, Joanne—merely lines written long ago by another Bill named Shakespeare——"

"Then quote correctly, Mr. Anson!"

"You left out the 'Oh', Nephew."

"So I did, Aunt, thanks for reminding me! So Mistress Joanne, with your kind attention I——"

"Not mine!" she retorted. "Yours is needed for the pigsties."

"And they shall have it anon, but now—

'Oh mistress mine, where are you roaming?
Oh stay and hear, your true love's coming,
That can sing both high and low;
Trip no further, pretty sweeting,
Journey's end in lover's meeting,
Every wise man's son doth know!'

So, mistress mine, most pretty sweeting, good night; may angels guard thy gentle slumber. Now, Bill, the pigsties!"

CHAPTER XVI

In Which Priscilla Pours Out Tea

"OH!" sighed Priscilla in a breathless rapture as her small hands wielded the out-of-doors teapot (rather unsteadily), for they were seated in a shady corner of the home meadow. "Oh, isn't everything splendid an' lovely, Anthony?"

"Yes," he answered, "almost!"

"Don't you miss your Auntie Joanne also, my dear?" enquired Aunt Jemima, busied as usual with her knitting.

"Yes, I do; only she would go riding—and in her bestest habit, too, though Anthony and I 'vited her so p'litely to have tea with us, but she wouldn't! Sometimes she's very on-ruly and more self-willed than me."

"You should say 'than I', Priscilla."

"Yes, but aren't I pouring our tea beautifully grand? Here's yours, Anthony!"

"Ladies first, sweetheart."

"Oh yes, I forgot—so you take it, Aunt 'Mima—and here's yours, Anthony; it's a bit full-up, so mind you don't spill it."

"And now," said Aunt Jemima, cup at lips, "talking of Sir Nicholas, Anthony——"

"Good Lord, Aunt, why of him?"

"Oh, Anthony," cried Priscilla reproachfully, "you've

been and gone and spilt it like I told you not! What made you so frightflee careless?"

"I wonder!" said Aunt Jemima, with one of her rare, gentle laughs. "Oh, Priscilla, my pet, we have actually forgotten that plum cake I baked for you. And please ask Ann to cut more bread and butter."

"Oh!" cried Priscilla, placing the teapot in safety. "Cake!" And away she sped.

"Yes," said Aunt Jemima placidly, "I have wondered quite often lately. Shall I tell you what about—who and why?"

"Please do."

"Well, I'm wondering just now if Sir Nicholas is at present residing in London or in the country—hereabout?"

"I believe—in the country."

"I'm also wondering if he is ever here at Fallowdene—in hobnailed boots?"

Nicholas laughed, at first ruefully, then with a sudden gladness, saying:

"A bull's-eye, Aunt, and I'm glad of it! But do please let me remain your 'Nephew Anthony' so long as I may."

"Of course, dear Nephew, of course! I would not spoil such a—hm—romantically sentimental situation, not I, indeed! But may I know why you came among us under a false name?"

"Not quite false, Aunt, because Anson was my mother's maiden name. I was an orphan child left to the care of my uncle, Sir Jonas, who cared so little for me that he packed me off straightway to a boarding school, and at holiday times, when I was compelled to stay at his town house or here at Grayladies, he avoided me as much as possible."

"So you lived at Grayladies?"

"Yes, that's one reason why I hate the place."

"Then you must have been the lonely boy I saw once or twice staring so wistfully between the bars of those great iron gates?"

"Yes, I was a somewhat desolate brat and, I suppose, pretty mischievous. It was at Grayladies that Uncle Jonas thrashed me with a horsewhip so that I could scarcely crawl to bed. Three days later I ran away to sea and, using my mother's name of Anson, was signed on as cabin boy. So a seaman I became, roving far and wide, but ended with a captain's ticket as first officer of the *Etruria* Indiaman."

"And you never saw your uncle again?"

"Never! Nor Grayladies either, until the other day."

"And yet he left you his enormous wealth!"

"Yes, to my amazement! And, considering the property isn't entailed, I'm still wondering why."

"Remorse perhaps for his harsh usage of you when a helpless child."

"Maybe, you gentle, kind-thinking aunt! However, I mean to use the money to some purpose."

"Which is perfectly evident, my dear!"

"But, Aunt Jemima, this purpose is not to buy Joanne— even if she could be bought—which she never could, of course, nor will I allow this confounded money to influence her choice! This is why I wish to remain her more or less humble handyman until, for love of Anthony Anson, she consents to be wed by Nicholas Harbourne. How say you, Aunt my dear?"

"That if Anthony plays his cards only half as well as

Nicholas did, then, soon or late, her beloved Anthony will see her loving and safe, in the arms of her adoring Nicholas."

"A right glorious thought, you most blessed of aunts! And may it be soon, for I—ah, yonder she comes! Back so soon and riding much too fast!"

"Then, dear me, she's in one of her tempests!"

"Tempests, Aunt?"

"Rageful tantrums, Nephew! You're surely aware how she flares and storms, all fire and fury one moment and sweet tranquillity the next? It is her fiery hair, I suppose."

"Such glorious hair!" said he, watching horse and rider gallop stablewards. "And when she rages, bless her, she only becomes the handsomer! The odd thing is, Aunt, it took me some little while to become aware how truly beautiful she is."

"Beautiful? Well—yes, I suppose she is—in a way."

"In every way!" said he with fervour. "Hers is that rare beauty that grows upon one. I mean, she seems more lovely every day, every hour."

"You must love her very truly, my dear?"

"Love her? Oh, Aunt, I adore her, and she knows it!"

"Have you told her so?"

"I've proposed to her!"

"How often?"

"Once."

"Lord Wolverton asks her every time they meet, and frequently."

"Wolverton's a clumsy fool!"

"But—a lord, my dear!"

"Certainly. But I'm as certain Joanne would never stoop to wed an oafish fool for his title."

"Anthony, I would not be too sure. She might wed the fool in a fury of pique or injured pride or desperation, or to spite herself, or to hurt her true love, or——"

"Oh, I say, Aunt, what frightful suggestions!"

"I say she might, Anthony, though I do not believe she would be such perfectly silly wretch. But it is as well to remember that old, disrespectful adage—'women be kittle cattle'. . . . And here comes your beauty, my dear, and looking beautifully sullen!"

Up rose Anthony, cup in hand, as with the long skirt of her riding-habit across her arm, my lady Sullen approached to enquire with most unexpected meekness:

"Am I too late to join you? If so, I will have my tea in the kitchen."

"This is our first," said Anthony, flourishing his cup in salutation, "so 'trip no further, pretty sweeting, your journey ends in lovers' meeting——'"

"It didn't!" she sighed. "My lord is away."

Anthony frowned (as she had expected), then laughed blithely and (to her indignant surprise) chanted:

"'Her lord's away, bravo, I say, hurrah hurray, there let him stay, for ever and aye, Joanne, I say, oh joyous day! So sit, I pray, and drink your tay. So ends my lay. And none so bad as lays go nowadays.' How say you, pretty sweeting?"

Joanne merely glanced towards him as she sank down, and with the utmost dignity, beside Aunt Jemima, who laughed with a serene enjoyment, saying:

I

"An excellent performance, Nephew. Indeed you retorted admirably and were quite lyrical besides!"

"So much so, Aunt, my dear, that I may probably indite an ode to my lady's eyebrow. Your left one, Joanne."

"What a ridiculous Mr. Anson you are!" said she, frowning, but with the dimple at her lips.

"And here is your tea, my poor, sweet child!" said Aunt Jemima. "Drink it and try to forget your bitter disappointment just for the present."

"What bitter—— Oh, you mean——" Joanne took a sip of tea very daintily and—smiled.

"Yes," said Aunt Jemima, smiling also. "It is marvellous what comfort there is in a cup of tea, Joanne; you become less doleful with every sip, I declare you do!"

"Oh, my darling, most perspicacious Aunt, the bitter disappointment you remarked in me was engendered of your own perfervid imagination entirely! And there, Aunt, is a sentence, a phrase or pronouncement which pleases me as entirely."

"Yes, my dear, it was a retort to me as excellent as Anthony's to you, though not so lyrical. It appears, then, that, although your lord was away, you do not exactly grieve his absence."

"No, Aunt. To tell you the truth I was quite relieved, because I hate the mere idea of having to thank Charles for anything, and I cannot think why."

"Because he is an arrogant gloater, Joanne, who would receive your thanks with the utmost condescension."

"Oh well, let's talk of cows instead. There are those eight beautiful Jerseys Mr. Bowyer offered me and at such a reasonable price, bless his kind heart! But I know we can't afford them at present, and when we can it will be too late, they will have been sold, and, oh, they are such lovely creatures!"

"My dear, we might borrow the money."

"Goodness, Aunt, who from?"

"Well, Elihu Dent helped us once before; then there are other old friends, Tom Bailey and John Martin——"

"And," said Anthony, "a well-meaning, clean, highly respectable, respectful, hard-working fellow named Anthony."

"You?" exclaimed Joanne, almost spilling her tea in surprise. "You, Mr. Anson?"

"No, merely Anthony."

"You really mean—oh, what do you mean?"

"That, being named Anthony, Anthony pray call me, then Anthony shall tell of Anthony something that may surprise and please you, I hope. So, Joanne, ask Anthony about Anthony, then listen to Anthony."

Joanne laughed at last, and instantly Sullen Gloom departed, as, with smiling submission, she enquired obediently:

"Please, Anthony, what does Anthony mean?"

"That owing to a lucky venture—on his last voyage— Anthony has a few hundred pounds, that Anthony will be most happy to lend at once any sum necessary and for any length of time."

"Good gracious!" she exclaimed, widening her beautiful eyes on him.

"Blue!" said he.

"Blue what?" she enquired.

"Your eyes, Joanne. They are a deep, dark blue—unless they're violet. I can never be quite sure. However, may I humbly suggest sending for those Jerseys before it is too late?"

"No, you may not, Mr.——"

"Say, 'Anthony'!"

"Very well, Anthony. I, and Aunt, of course, are very grateful for your kind offer, but I must not send for those lovely cows because I cannot borrow so much money from you or——"

"Why not, Joanne?"

"Well—because——"

"Because—what?"

"Oh, just because."

"That is no answer, Joanne."

"Then I—although so very grateful, I must refuse to be under such obligation to—our handyman."

"How absurd!" he exclaimed. "And how very ungenerous of you!"

"Ungenerous? Of me?"

"Yes, to deny me this pleasure. To refuse an offer so humbly well-meant. I only hope Aunt Jemima will be kinder and more understanding."

"Yes, Nephew," she answered, "I can, I will, and I do. For, besides being Joanne's perspicacious Aunt, I am her partner as well. So I accept your offer thankfully——"

At this moment Priscilla reappeared carrying, and with elaborate care, a large platter on which were dark, odd-shaped lumps of what had been a rich fruit-cake, thus she approached, saying in woeful accents:

"Oh, Aunt 'Mima, I'm 'fraid this lovely cake has been and broke itself a bit, and it only slipped off the plate once! I've took all this while trying to mend it, but it won't stick together again. So please axcuse me and forgive me and 'low me to ampologise. If you'll be so o-bleeging, dear Aunt."

"Of course I will, my pet! Sit down and have your tea."

"Yes, I will, Aunt, and thank you for being so 'dorable kind to me." So saying, down she sat close beside Anthony to proffer him a special piece of cake with the assurance:

"Take this lump because it's the cleanest; I wiped the dust off it for you frightflee carefully, my Anthony."

"Thank you, my Priscilla," said he and, taking this particular lump, ate it with very evident enjoyment, being watched anxiously by Priscilla, who enquired:

"It isn't very gritty, is it?"

"Not a bit, sweetheart, except here and there."

Now chancing to meet Joanne's gaze, he saw in her eyes such look that for the moment he forgot all else, thrilled by the glad and wholly unexpected wonder of it, and when she spoke it was in tone that matched her look:

"Sometimes I admire you greatly—Anthony!"

Thus they gazed on one another until she, in turn, becoming aware of the adoration in his eyes, flushed, sighed and turned from him to enquire:

"Do you really mean to buy those cows, Aunt?"

"Ooh, more cows?" cried Priscilla.

"That is for Aunt to say, dear."

"Well, say yes, Aunt 'Mima, 'cause I like cows when they aren't bulls. And I don't mind bulls—much, when

I've got my Anthony to save me nice and safe, like he did."

"Yes," said Joanne, shuddering, "it was very wonderful, but horrible. Oh, terrible! I have often wondered just how you did it—Anthony?"

"Sheer luck, oh mistress mine, and pray remark the 'Oh'! And may I have another cup of tea, Aunt Jemima? And shall you buy those cows?"

"Oh yes, I shall send for them this very afternoon."

"They will cost a great deal," sighed Joanne, mournfully, "and when and how can we hope to repay the money?"

"In good time, my dear," replied Aunt Jemima placidly. "With this splendid herd we can afford to market some of our own stock. So, my dear, the sooner we let Will Bowyer know, the better."

"Very well, Aunt, I'll send George and Bill at once," said Joanne, rising.

"Good!" exclaimed Nicholas; then, gulping his tea, he rose also, enquiring rather wistfully:

"May I go with you——"

CHAPTER XVII

Gives Some Description of a Kiss

AND so together, side by side, they crossed the broad home meadow, walking very sedately and both unwontedly silent, until Nicholas, finding her so demurely aloof, enquired suddenly at last:

"Oh, mistress mine, pray what of the home you are to make for me someday, somewhere, if I present you with the wherewithal, a house, furniture and so on? For the more I see of you, the more impatient I grow for the day when——"

"Mr. Anson," she exclaimed indignantly, "you take too much for granted!"

"And yet," said he, "all I desire of you or beg of life to grant me is just one only woman of all the teeming millions—merely you, Joanne."

"Oh? And why—merely me?" she enquired, and slowed her step, waiting the one and only answer. But though Nicholas was, in many ways, a truly handy man, yet being quite unversed in the complexities of a woman's mind, or rather such proudly shy, delicate woman as Joanne, he now (instead of uttering that one essential word) replied with a serene and therefore irritating assurance:

"Because we were, and are, destined for one another. I

knew myself wholly yours and you as completely mine in that first hour we met."

"Did you indeed, sir!"

"Oh yes, I was perfectly certain! I knew by instinct we were, and are, fated to unite. And when you had ridden away I——"

"Guzzled ale from a pewter pot!" she snapped, with show of white teeth and halting the better to scorn him.

"Why yes," he admitted, halting also, "yes, I finished my ale, naturally, but——"

"And just as naturally, Mr. Anthony Anson, your animal-like instinct led you entirely astray! You are—not mine! I—I don't want you and won't have you; most—certainly—not! As for me being yours because of destiny—such nonsense—I never shall be! Oh no! I am my own, thank heaven! And as for your 'destiny'—I defy it, yes, and snap my fingers at your 'fate'—like this!" And she did so (gracefully, of course), but with gesture so fiercely determined that—down fell part of her long habit to lie quite unnoticed. Thus when (and with superb dignity) she made to walk on again, her foot caught in it so that she tripped and would have fallen but for the ready arm of watchful Nicholas, who instantly and in an easy, casual manner, took her in both arms, drew her to his breast, and kissed her in a manner anything but casual; and then, to his blissful astonishment, felt her lips respond to his—for one rapturous moment only, then, feeling how desperately she struggled, he freed her, stepped back and stood awed and spellbound while Joanne —as Aunt Jemima would have said—flared and flamed in one of her most tempestuous tantrums. . . . And when she had told him, with many and divers adjectives, precisely what kind of a brute-beast he was, she became by degrees plaintively reproachful, plying him with such questions as:

"How dared you? How could you be so cruel—to take such hateful advantage of me? Oh why—why did you?" And this she asked almost pleadingly. And again, instead of giving the right answer, he replied:

"Because you are Joanne."

At this she flared anew, demanding, bitterly scornful:

"Was that—that kiss snatched from my helplessness in part payment of our debt, Aunt's and mine—was it? Because if so I——"

She stopped and caught her breath, for now she beheld an anger that quelled her own, a cold fury so sudden and terrible that it frightened her, or very nearly; and when Nicholas spoke it was in tone hushed though dreadful as his look.

"Joanne, for the damnable injustice of that question you deserve to—suffer!" Uttering the word, he snatched her up in arms that crushed her to helplessness, and, with her thus, began to walk slowly down the lane while she, gazing up into this face so direly altered, yet ventured speech, though very humbly:

"Won't you please—put me down?"

"Not me, Mistress Jo," he answered somewhat breathlessly. "Why for should I? Though, e'cod, you'm no feather!"

"Suppose the men—or anyone see——"

"Them be arl in rickyard, marm, and us be in shady lane." Here, to her relief, he laughed, though rather fiercely, and became again almost the Anthony she knew.

"Where are you taking me, pray?"

"To the rickyard, of course."

"Then for mercy's sake—set me down."

"In-deed," said he, more breathlessly then ever, "I should like to—in a way, for you weigh more—every moment. Because, Joanne, thank heaven—you are most —deliciously buxom!"

"Oh, what a hideous thing to say of me!"

"Ah, but what—a lovely truth—to know of you!"

"Well, put me down before you drop me."

"Never, oh—mistress mine, until—you ask meekly, sweetly—and properly."

"How must I ask?"

"You must—say in your gentlest voice— 'Dearest of all Anthonys, instead of bearing me—upon your heart, let me—walk beside you—all the way, but always—keep me in your heart."

"But what a ridiculous thing to say!"

"However, Joanne, you—had better say it—at once, because in—another minute we—shall be with—Bill and George and old Joe! Listen, you—can hear their voices——"

"Oh, then please let me walk beside you—dearest of all Anthonys. Oh, I could bite you!"

"Gentlest of all Joannes, I quite believe it. There! Let your pretty feet go beside me now and—to the end of life's journey."

And presently, walking side by side and very sedately,

they entered the spacious rickyard; and never had Joanne seemed more charmingly demure or dignified, as:

"Oh, Bill," said she, speaking royally, "we have decided to buy those eight Jerseys and think you had better go for them at once."

"And by Goles," he exclaimed joyfully, "ee couldn't nowise do no better, Mistus Jo, no—how! They cows be cows sure-ly, wi' udders onto 'em like beeloons, ar, so tight as drums! Eh, Jarge?"

"Ar, lovely they be!"

"Eyes never see none better, no question!" piped old Joe.

"So, marm, me and Jarge'll go for 'em drackly minute——"

"And I'll along wi' ee!" quoth Joe.

"No need for to trouble they old legs o' yourn, Joe, so doddlish as they be, so whyfor will ee trouble em, Joe?"

"My old legs don't trouble me none, my lad, so don't ee trouble for they; and, doddlish or no, I be agoin' long of ee."

"And now," said Joanne, as the faithful three trudged away together, arguing like the good old friends they were, "now I'll bid you good evening. It will be a far better evening for me when your loan is repaid, this debt we should not have incurred. I shall find it a heavy burden and shall free myself of it soon as possible, you may be sure."

"Oh, I am," he sighed, "because you are, I repeat, so very selfish, Joanne, to deny me this small pleasure. But, talking of burdens: if there is any chance those long skirts may trip you again, I'll burden myself with your comely though cumbersome bux——"

"You are," said she, "a hateful man!"

"And you," sighed he, "a weightful Joanne!"

"Oh——!" she exclaimed furiously and left him.

"Ah!" he murmured tenderly, and watched her out of sight, ere he went his solitary way.

CHAPTER XVIII

Tells How Nicholas Met an Old Shipmate

NOW AS Nicholas trudged villagewards through a fragrant gloaming, he beheld a man who leaned upon a somewhat rickety gate staring very earnestly at the smallish, desolate farmhouse, whose latticed windows stared back, from rooms where life was not, upon an untended garden where weeds flourished in tangled riot.

As Nicholas approached, this man turned, and thus showed a bronzed visage, which, though somewhat weatherbeaten like the house, was lit by kindly blue eyes and adorned by a pair of neatly trimmed whiskers.

"Sir," he began; then, noticing the hobnailed boots and gaiters, paused uncertainly. But his keen glance travelling up from these to their wearer's clean-cut, aquiline face with its unconscious air of command, this fellow snatched off his hat the better to knuckle bristly eyebrow, saying:

"Sir, I can't be mistook—you're Mr. Anson, first officer o' the *Etruria,* or sink me!"

"And you," said Nicholas, "by all that's wonderful, you're Bob Travis, the hardy old shell-back who, long before the *Etruria,* taught me more real seamanship than all the books——"

"Which you, sir, were mighty quick to larn."

"Bob, old shipmate, shake hands! We weathered many a gale together, you and I."

"Ay, sir. D'ye mind that time off the Horn—'twere blowing a bit and our fore-topmast carried away and you and me and poor Tom Pell went aloft to cut away the wreckage and poor Tom were blowed overboard and you, trying for to save him, nigh went, too?"

"Yes, by Jingo! I shouldn't be here but for you, Bob."

"Ay—caught ye by luck and y'r belt, I did, just as you went."

"And hauled me back to safety and life, Bob!"

"And the time we shipped them mutinous raskells at Austrayley and you did more ag'in 'em wi' fist and marlinspike than the cap'n wi' his revolver."

"You did your share, Bob!"

"Ay, sir. But b'glory—how you loved a fight!"

"I was younger then, messmate. But what are you doing hereabouts?"

"Why, sir, me having quit the sea, swaller'd the anchor, cable and all, I'm cruising about to find some snug berth for a final anchorage, where me and my wife Soo can bring to for good and all. Y'see, Mr. Anson, I'm Sussex born, and bred to farming and, b'glory, I love the land, and no place better than this here! I were thinking as you hove alongside as how this little old place would soot me and my Soo and brother Ben right perfect. You'll mind Ben as were bosun's mate aboard the *Etruria*?"

"Of course! A smart sailorman. Has he quit the sea also?"

"Ay, and wants for to come afarming along o' me, sir."

"And you think this place might suit you?"

"Sir, I'm mighty sartin-sure it would. I've took the liberty o' looking it over, so if it can be bought——"

"No, I'm sure it can't. But you could have it on lease, Bob, long as you will, and—at extremely modest rental—at least so I believe."

"That 'ud soot us right noble, Mr. Anson, ay, b'glory! Who owns it, sir, and how do I set about speaking to him?"

"It belongs to a fellow named Sir Nicholas Harbourne, Bob, and you will have to see his lawyers in London."

"I'll bear away bright and early tomorrer, sir, if you'll be s' good to lay me a course, give me my bearings how to fetch up with 'em."

"Old shipmate, I'll do better. I'll write you a letter to 'em if you'll bear away with me to my lodgings and drink a pint of ripe old stingo while I'm busy with pen and ink."

"Ay ay, sir, and I'll be main grateful, Mr. Anson."

"And yonder, Bob, bearing about three points to starboard, is the Soaring Lark, kept by Bo'sun Will, an old Navy man, so mind your eye—come and meet him."

Thus presently, while these two old seadogs talked ships and the seven seas, Nicholas, seated aloft in his cosy bed-sitting-room, indited the following letter:

"June 26, 18—

"To Messrs. Biggs, Dyke and Biggs.
"Gent:
"You will lease the farm, known as Willowbrook, to the bearer, Mr. Robert Travis, for such term as he

desires at the rental of (£30) thirty pounds p.a. and oblige.

"Yours truly,

"Nicholas Harbourne."

CHAPTER XIX

In Which Nicholas, Building Pigsties, Versifies

THE EIGHT Jerseys, paid for a week ago and now settled in bovine content, were proving their worth even more copiously than expected, as Joanne was being informed (yet again) by old Joe, her aged cowman, wise by long and varied experience:

"Booties they be, Miss Joanne, I tell ee, ar, that they be! The gallons as they do give so free and kind do warm me 'eart, it do——"

"Yes, Joe, they were a bargain. But has Bill returned from market?"

"Ar, I be'leeve so, and their milk s' rich in cream, they'm quality, no question!"

"But why hasn't Bill reported to me? Do you know if he sold all the lambs and bullocks?"

"Ar, so I do think, Miss Jo—'owsever, 'e come back wi'out ever a critter——"

"Well, where is he?"

"Downalong by they pigsties talkin' wi' Mist' Anthony, I rackon."

So to the pigsties went Joanne and here beheld Bill in earnest converse with Nicholas who was busied with trowel and plumb-line.

"Whatever are you doing here, Bill?" she demanded.

"You know how anxious I am about our stock. Did you sell—all?"

"Ay, Mistus Jo, I did!" he answered, leaning on his long drover's stick.

"Well?"

"Well, I shouldn't 'ardly call it well, Miss Jo. No, I should say 'twere middling fair like. You says 'sell', you says, so sell 'em I did and—yere be the money!"

"Oh!" she exclaimed, counting hastily. "Oh, Bill— is this—all?"

"Ar, every farden, Miss Jo, and I do wish 'twere more, but the bidding was sap-rising low, ar, 'twere a poor market for sure."

"But those bullocks were in prime condition, Bill, and the lambs some of our best."

"Mistus Jo, ee must know as, though ourn were good, there was others better and fetched better money, nat'rally."

"Then I—oh, I wish we hadn't sold!"

"So do I, Mistus! But sell you tells and sell I did according."

"Yes, yes, of course!" she sighed. "But I had hoped for so much more."

"So did I, Miss Jo, till I see they others! Mr. Bailey's Southdowns topped the bidding, and no wonder—he don't never breed but from the very best."

"Oh well, never mind, Bill!" said she, with pitiful attempt at a smile. "I suppose it might have been worse —though I—hardly think so, and I dared to believe this was going to be such a—glad summer!" Then she turned from them suddenly, and, if her step was unwontedly slow, her head was upborne, bravely as ever.

"Ar," sighed Bill dismally, "yon goes disapp'intment on two pretty legs, Mist' Anthony; they was tears in they bootiful eyes, and no wonder, con-siderin'! Doleful, sir, doleful!"

"Yes!" said Nicholas, plying his trowel quite viciously. "Farming seems a pretty cursed business for a woman, Bill!"

"Ar, or a man, sir! Wot wi' the bot, foot and mouth, scab, footrot, murrian, glanders and I dunno wot all— not t' mention failure o' root and standing crops! I rackon farmin' be a powerful man's job——"

"Or a very brave woman's, Bill!"

"And b'goles, Mist' Anthony, there never were no braver woman ever drawed breath than our Mistus Joanne, so says me and Jarge and old Joe, and I rackon us knows by ax-perience."

"And very faithful you've been all three, fair weather and foul; yes, a mighty help by all accounts! And because I am anxious to help also, I want you trusty three to know I'm with you to help in any and every way I can. Is this understood, Bill, old fellow? I mean, will you teach me to use a scythe and a pitchfork properly and so on."

"Sir, I says ar and wi' arl my 'eart, and so'll say the three on us, being now four on us. So arl as I can say be this——"

"An—toe—nee!" Towards them, across the wide home meadow, Priscilla came speeding on those little nimble feet of hers, hair and sunbonnet flying as usual.

"Ar!" nodded Bill. "But wot I now says, sir, is as any man as can win the innocent 'eart o' such a package o' sweetness as Miss Priss is a man as it do honour me for to know!" So saying, he saluted Priscilla with prodigious flourish of his long drover's prod and trudged away.

"Ooh, Anthony," gasped Priscilla, breathless with haste and admiration, "what a bee-ootiful pigsty you're making! I hope our pigs, when they come, 'll 'preciate such a lovely house. I love pigs, don't you?"

"I do, sweetheart, especially when they're nice and clean and pink . . . or properly roasted with lots of crackling."

"Anthony, it's so lovely how we love the same things, because I like crackling, too, with lots of apple sauce, you know."

"Yes, by Jingo, I forgot the apple sauce and sage and onions."

"I can eat apple sauce all by itself. Ah, but now I'm going to tell you. Today in school I sur-prised myself with my own cleverness by making up a word for you and me—listen to it: 'Splendorious!' Now isn't that fine?"

"Gloriously splendid, my precious."

"I'm glad you 'preciate it, because that's what you are, my splendorious Anthony. But now I've got to tell you something doleful. All the children at school and everywhere have got lots of uncles and I haven't a single one, and that's doleful, no question, Anthony, isn't it? So what can us do about it?"

"Us can't, sweetheart, nowise—without your Auntie Jo's help—she could find you one. Yes, you might ask her to give you a nice, loving, obedient uncle."

"So I will, and I do hope she will. And tonight my nasty homework's sums again, long division, and they're always so hatefully long and always divide wrong. Ooh, that was poetry—'long' and 'wrong'. I've took to making poetry; I made some today in the jogafree lesson, all about you and me. Would you like to hear it?"

"I should indeed, my precious one."

"Well, you shall, if you'll let me slap a bit of mortar about like you do and stick a brick in it—and there's a bit more poitry, 'stick' and 'brick', so will you, please, Anthony—dear?"

"If you'll take care not to spoil that pretty little frock."

"Do you think it's pretty?"

"Of course I do. It's a lovely frock!"

"Now I'm loving you for loving my frock, Anthony, because I'm in it—and I'll be most aw-flee careful."

"Very well then. In this mortar you may stick, for your Anthony, this brick—if you'll promise to take care you won't get mortar in your hair, or, my sweetheart, let it mess and spoil your very pretty dress."

Now at this she gazed up at him in such wide-eyed, rapturous wonder that he stooped and kissed her.

"Oh, my Anthony," she murmured, "that was—splendorious, and so are you—to make poitry as well as pigsties! So now, before I stick a brick—I'll read you mine; I've wrote it into my 'rithmetick book and here it be, so be you listening, please?"

"With both ears, my darling."

And so, in her clear, sweet young voice, Priscilla read aloud:

" 'I'll always love my Anto-nee beecause my Anthony loves me. So when my Anthony I see, his sweetheart I shall always be. And I love frogs and so does he. And after we have had our tea, he'll help me with my jogafree' —only tonight it isn't jogafree, but it had to be to make it sound right. Do you like it?"

"Splendoriously, sweetheart! Every rhyme is perfect and—oho, yonder now comes your Aunt Jo, so if you wish to stick a brick, my precious, you had best be quick."

Thus when Joanne reached them she beheld her small niece extremely busy with mortar and trowel.

"Good gracious!" she exclaimed. "What on earth——"

"Pigsties, my lady!" quoth Nicholas. "We are constructing this range of piggish homes and building love into them with every brick. Thus these will be truly the very loveliest of piggeries."

"I'm afraid it will be a long time before we have any pigs to grunt in them," sighed Joanne.

"Why not, Auntee Jo?"

"Because money doesn't grow on trees, my dear."

"However," said Nicholas, "I must advise you, oh mistress mine; there has been mention of—an uncle."

"What uncle, and whose?"

"The uncle who should be, is not, and yet may be—we hope! Don't us, my precious?"

"Yes," she answered, still busied with her enthralling task, "us do, sure-ly—no question!"

"Priscilla, speak properly."

"Well, but I'm only talking like our Bill do, and Joe and——"

"Well—don't!"

"Very well, Auntie Joe, and I've sticked the brick. Anthony, will it do?"

"Splendoriously!" he replied, relieving her of the heavy trowel.

"Oh, Anthony, the way you say it makes it beeootifully grander; it's a word I made up, Auntie Jo, and it minds me to ask you for my uncle."

"But you haven't one and——"

"I know, and that's what's so doleful, so I want you please to get me one."

"Oh!" murmured Joanne, glancing askance at Nicholas, who was hard at work again. "Do you indeed, miss!"

"Yes, Auntie dear, indeed I do—a nice big strong one like my Anthony what'll be kind and 'bedient like my Anthony."

"I see! And did your Anthony suggest him-self, my dear?"

"Madam," said Nicholas, tapping a brick firmly into place, "certainly not! But your beloved small niece informs me that all other little girls have uncles galore and that you should allow her to be the exception strikes me as pitiful, shameful and not to be endured——"

"Ridiculous!" exclaimed Joanne, dimpling.

"Doleful, marm, doleful!" he retorted. "Why should our Priscilla go un-uncled, when you might so soon and so easily satisfy her very proper and praiseworthy avuncular craving?"

"However, Mr. Anthony, sir, I came merely to inform you Aunt Jemima expects you to tea which will be ready very soon——"

"Ooh, Auntie Jo, and what I forgot to tell you is what

makes him so 'stremely splendorious is—besides making lovely pigs'-houses he can make poitry, too, so Anthony will you make some about Auntie Jo—can you?"

"Certainly—after a fashion, my precious. For instance, when your aunt is near—I mean your dear Aunt Jo, my dear—all things more beautiful appear; this lovely world now, if she will, she can, for us, make lovelier still."

"Oh," cried Priscilla, clasping her small hands in ecstasy, "he's growing splendoriouser, isn't he, Auntie Jo?"

"Yes," she laughed. "You had better bring him into tea before he becomes too splendorious."

"Well then, you bring him, too. Take his other hand, please, Auntie."

Now seeing how Joanne hesitated, Nicholas shook his head, saying gravely:

"No, sweetheart, she didn't oughter, until I've washed away this mortar; but then, Priscilla, if she will, my hand is hers to hold until——"

"Oh!" exclaimed Joanne, frowning and yet with irrepressible laugh which on any other lips would certainly have been a giggle. "Oh, come in to tea!"

CHAPTER XX

Concerning the Beauties in Haymaking

THUS SPED these happy days, lengthening to ever happier weeks (for Nicholas, at least), though everywhere upon this wide estate of Harbourne was a pervading content that was to make this a truly glad summer.

Indeed, upon this particular afternoon the fragrant air was glad with voices and laughter where the haymakers, men and women, wrought with rake and pitchfork, and not one of them seemed lighter of heart, more nimble of pretty foot or dexterous of slim, sunburnt hand than "Mistus Joanne"; her detested reddish hair was eclipsed for the time being in deep, shady sunbonnet, her lithe form clad in simple gown that, with her every graceful movement, showed the lovely shape of her as she plied pitchfork with quite astonishing ease, saying to her somewhat unhandyman who laboured close by:

"Watch now! Like—this!" Here with skilled thrust and twist of pitchfork she hoisted a great pile of fragrant, golden hay to George who stood perched aloft on the great sky-blue wain mounted upon its enormous pink wheels. Now turning very suddenly upon her handyman and perceiving how and where he looked:

"Miss-ter Anthony," she hissed, "what are you—goggling at?"

"Goggling? Am I?"

"Yes, like a fish! Was it at my pitchfork or—me?"

"Certainly, marm!"

"Which?"

"Both, Miss Jo. I gaze in awe upon your pitchfork; I watch, entranced, the gracious swing and sway of you—those slender hands that seem quite unfit for such toil yet which make toil a joy to behold, those arms so sweetly, smoothly round and dazzling white where Old Sol hasn't kissed them so fervently—and all the charm——"

"Miss-ter Anthony, I think, no, I'm sure, you had better go and work over yonder with old Joe!"

"A grand old chap 'e be, Mistus, true Sussex sure-ly; 'owsever, I prefers to bide along of ee, marm, no question." Here, meaning to frown, she smiled instead, that is to say, her ruddy lips quivered till beside them came the dimple he so loved to see because it appeared all too rarely, and which he yearned to kiss so greatly that instead he pitchforked, tossing hay up at George with such speed and violence that, being on the receiving end, George cried:

"Easy, Mist' Anthony! Don't ee fork s' wild like or ee'll be aprongin' of I, which'll be sad for I, sure-ly!"

"My humblest apologies, George, old boy. I fancy I'd better try a rake instead."

"Ar, 'twill be a mite less perilsome, sir, I do rackon." So saying, George nodded, chirruped to his horses and the great wagon creaked and jolted to where the next load awaited him.

"I'm wondering," said Joanne, glancing anxiously across meadow and cornfield towards the dusty, tree-shaded highroad, "what can be keeping Bill and how the market went today."

"So am I!" said Nicholas. "Though my wonder is why, after your last disappointment, you ventured to sell more of your stock?"

"Because I can't bear to owe money or lie under an obligation to anyone, Anthony—more especially Mr. Anson."

"What utter nonsense, Joanne! And why 'specially' this Anson fellow, why?"

"Because!" she sighed.

"If that is your best answer, mistress, I'll propound a better. Because you either hate the miserable wretch, this well-meaning handyman of yours, or love the happiest fellow in all this lovely world. The question is, which? And this you only can answer. So, Joanne . . . my dear . . . will you answer?"

"No!" said she, gently though with the utmost finality. "Not until"—here she turned so that the deep sunbonnet quite hid her face—"such question is asked . . . in the . . . only right and proper way."

"Then, oh my dear, tell me how and I'll ask, beg, sue and plead here and now—if you will—upon my knees! Shall I kneel?"

"Idiot—no! With so many eyes to see us!"

"Eyes or no, kneel I will unless you tell me precisely——"

"An—toe—nee!"

"Thank heaven!" sighed Joanne. "Here comes your small, pertinacious 'sweetheart' to relieve me of her more pertinacious Anthony!"

"I love to hear and watch you speak my name, Joanne!"

"What do you mean by 'watch', pray?"

"Your lips—you have the loveliest mouth, Joanne—your lips are even more beautiful when they utter my name, especially the 'tony' part." Here once again these same lovely lips quivered to a smile; then, throwing back her head, Joanne laughed—at the which unwonted sound:

"Ooh!" gasped Priscilla, breathless with speed and astonishment. "Auntie Jo, you're—axe-stually laughing and . . . you do it so . . . nice and proper . . . it do make ee prettier . . . than ever . . . it do, no question. . . . So I be awondering why . . . you don't do it . . . oftener, I be."

"Gracious goodness, child! You must—not—speak as the village children do——"

"Oh, but I don't . . . I only talk a bit like Bill and George and Joe do, and I like them lots because they're all dears and nice, they be."

"Yes, I know they are. But you must always remember you are a little lady and behave as such."

"Does that mean like you, 'cause you're a lady?"

"Well—yes."

"Then that'll be fright-flee awful!"

"Oh, why, miss?"

"Cause if I bee-have like you I mustn't ever kiss my Anthony, like you don't! And, please, why don't you? Aunt Mima does; I caught her at it once—doesn't she, Anthony?"

"She does, sweetheart, bless her! Because, you see, aunts usually kiss their nephews."

"Well, if she does, why don't you, Auntie Jo?"

"Because I am not your Anthony's aunt—by adoption! And because, being myself, I have no desire to kiss your Anthony. And if you go on asking silly questions I—I shall take you indoors—to bed, miss!"

"That would be horrible cruel for any nice child, wouldn't it, Anthony?"

"So very horrible, sweetheart, that your beloved aunt couldn't and wouldn't—on such a glorious afternoon, with all this lovely hay for us to rake. And, of course, she ought to kiss me quite frequently, considering!"

"Considering what, if you please?" Joanne demanded, handling her pitchfork threateningly.

"Considering, most precious 'sweeting', we were made for each other—to have and to hold 'till death do us part —which it never shall."

"Ooh!" cried Priscilla again. "Do that mean wedlock's holy bond, like Ann says shall make her and George one, do it?"

"Hush!" exclaimed Joanne, thrusting her pitchfork into the nearest hay-pile quite viciously. "Ann ought not to tell of—of such matters to a child like you."

"Oh, she didn't! She telled it to Nancy in the dairy, only I was there and heard."

"You hear a great deal too much, child!" said Joanne, her anxious gaze towards the distant road again.

"However," sighed Nicholas, "it is my earnest hope that someday wedlock's holy bond may shackle and unite me with——"

"At last!" said Joanne and hurried away to meet Bill, who had just entered the hayfield.

"Sometimes," said Priscilla, thoughtfully, "I'm 'fraid

she doesn't like you, Anthony, but sometimes I think she do."

"Ah, why, my precious?"

"Because when she sees you looking at her so kind-like, she frowns, and when you don't, she doesn't, but looks at you kind-like, too."

"Now for that, sweetheart, I'm going to kiss you."

"And that," said Priscilla, after he had done so, "that's pre-zackly what Auntie Jo said the other night when she axed me why I loved you so much, and I said because you were my Anthony, only she kissed me twice—hard! And when I asked why, she said because I was such a faithful little soul, and when I wanted to know why, she blowed out the candles and left me in the dark, only I didn't mind because the moon shined on me so bright. I love the moon, don't you?"

"Yes, my dear, I do."

"And when it's big and round I can see a lady's face, sideways. Have you seen her?"

"Often, sweetheart. Yes, the moon is a very kind and gentle lady."

"And now, Anthony, I think we'll do a bit of raking, shall us? Oh, but us can't 'cause there goes the bell for tea. Come 'long!"

So, hand in hand, they crossed the hayfield to a shady corner where a long trestle-table had been set with a plenteous repast presided over by Ann, who, curtsying demurely, said:

"If you please, sir, Miss Jemima is expecting of you indoors for tea. Miss Priss, you are to bide and help me look after our haymakers."

"Ooh, and will you 'llow me to pour out tea, Ann dear?"

"If you'll be very careful, Miss Priss. . . ."

But as Nicholas, on his way towards the house, turned into the stableyard, he beheld old Joe, head bared respectfully, gazing up at Lord Wolverton, who, gallantly mounted astride noble horse, was resplendent in boots, buckskins and hunting pink, wherefore Nicholas pulled down the brim of his own weatherbeaten hat and, making the most of his hobnailed boots, clattered forward to demand in speech matching his attire:

"Wot do gen'leman want of ee, Joe?"

"Yere be 'is ludship axin' for Mistus Joanne——"

"Oh, ar? Then tell 'im 'er be gone to Jee-roosa-lem or Timmybucktoo."

"Eh?" exclaimed my lord angrily. "What's that?"

"Lord, you 'eered me, I rackon. 'Owsever, Joe, tell 'im as 'ow our mistus don't want never no lords nor sich 'ere-along, and no more don't us. So, ho, Joe, tell 'im t' go!"

"Ha, you infernally impudent yokelly blackguard!" cried my lord, flourishing his heavy riding-crop; but a pitchfork being within reach, Nicholas took it up and, thus armed, fronted that threatening whip.

"Oh, Joe," said he, brandishing the pitchfork, "tell the gen'leman to sheer off afore 'e runs foul of these yere prongs."

Old Joe merely goggled and gasped, but Lord Wolverton reining back before this two-pointed threat, and dumb with a fury beyond utterance, wheeled his trampling horse and galloped out of the yard.

"Eh—my soul!" piped Old Joe. "And him the Lord Charles!" Nicholas laughed and, setting by the pitchfork, went his way very happily, until, passing the great tithe-barn, he espied Bill perched mournfully upon a shaft of the gig, a drooping, disconsolate figure.

"Why so mournful, Bill?" he enquired. "What's wrong?"

"Me, sir, Miss Jo, and they cattle! Last week I sold 'em wrong according to her; today I brings 'em back and does wrong again so doin', says she. Lordy, there bean't no pleasing of 'er no 'ow and no when—gimme a fine dish o' tongue, she did! But wot was a man to do when prices was so danged low?"

"Wait for a better market, as you did, and very wisely, old fellow."

"Ay, sir, but she don't think so."

"She will, later on, Bill. Meanwhile our little Priscilla is waiting to comfort and cheer you with tea and cake in the hayfield, so off with you!"

"Ah, Miss Priss, Lord bless her li'l 'eart, for comfort me she do and 'ave done ever since she were born into this yere world o' trouble and——"

"Oh, Charles," cried a voice in joyful greeting, "how glad I am to see you——"

" 'Tis mistus!" whispered Bill, ducking back into the shadowy barn. "Miss Jo—and along o' Lord Wolverton, dannel him!"

"Ay ay, Bill, dannel him twice!" murmured Nicholas, retreating also into this fragrant gloom.

"Yes, Charles, my dear," said Joanne, rather loudly and pausing nearby to say it, "I want to thank you for your letter and its . . . precious enclosure . . . but, oh, Charles, my dear lord, I am—still so much surprised by your unexpected goodness and generosity that I don't know how to thank you properly."

"There are ways, m'dear—delicious ways, several in fact, that lovely woman may show her gratitude, eh, Jo, eh? As for the I.O.U., I merely held it hoping to give it you for a wedding present, one of many. But now, m'dearest, if you are so truly grateful—show it, ha yes— prove it to me by using that most lovely mouth, these delicious lips, in far sweeter way than speech. Come, why not, m'dearest lovely?"

"Because, as you know, I hate being kissed, Charles, and shall never kiss any man except—the one!"

"Well, aren't I that man, your man, m'dear, the one and only? I must be, I will be, I am! So, my bewitching tantalisation, come to——"

"Charles, don't be so ridiculous! Instead go with me indoors to Aunt Jemima and tea."

"Not I! Oh no, I want neither; all I desire is you! You here alone as you are, you in my arms—like this——"

"Charles, don't—don't be revolting!"

"You, Joanne, all the delicious provocation of you, here close in my grasp——"

"Charles—my lord——"

"Your lips on mine!"

"No—no! Oh—horrid——"

"Like this, Joanne, and—this——"

"Oh, nauseous! You've been drinking! Let me go— ah, you—you must be drunk!"

L

Scarcely was this word uttered than from out of the barn issued a voice singing an old sea shanty that demanded in words slightly altered for the occasion:

" 'Wot's to be done wi' the drunken man now?
    Wot's to be done wi' this drunken chap, now?
    Wot's to be done wi' this drunken lord, now?
    Er–lie in the mornin'?'

Ho, Bill, gimme a hand wi' this gig. . . . So it's

    'Wey–hey hup she rises,
    Wey–hey hup she rises,
    Wey–hey hup she rises,
    Er–lie in the mornin'.' "

Here, to the accompaniment of this chant and with grind of its iron-shod wheels, forth rolled the gig urged by the singer in such manner that Lord Wolverton was compelled to sudden violent exertion, a backward, sideways leap.

"Damnation!" he panted viciously as he caught and steadied his toppling hat.

"Charles, do—not—swear!" cried Joanne indignantly, but with certain dimple very much in evidence.

"But what the devil—who—ah! So it's you again, is it, you infernally insolent, clumsy bumpkin?"

"Ay, sir," replied Nicholas, setting down the gig-shafts to touch his low-drawn hat very respectfully, "it be only I."

"Then be off before I make you feel my boot! Get

out, d'ye hear—or must I kick you back to your native dunghill——"

"For shame, Charles! Be silent and——"

"But this—this loutish bumpkin is so persistently insolent."

"Nonsense!" said Joanne (still dimpling). "You are over-sensitive and too imaginative, though I never thought so until now."

"Ah—now," said my lord, between his teeth, "if only I had my whip."

"Nonsense!" said Joanne (still dimpling). "You are here where my men are working, so give me your arm and let us go." Scowling, he obeyed and was led away still maundering for his whip.

Then Nicholas chuckled, while Bill bent himself double with suppressed laughter.

"Lordy—lordy!" he wheezed when they were alone. "You very nigh run my lordship down."

"I did my best, Bill."

"Ar, sure-ly! If 'e 'adn't been so spry as a goat you'd ha' got 'im, no question!"

"And a 'goat' describes my lord so well, I grieve to have missed him."

"So do I, sir, uncommon grieved I be."

"However, let us temper our disappointment with tea —though first help me back with this well-meant gig." So, with sundry "Yo-ho, hup she rises," and other nautical aids to bodily effort, the vehicle was rolled back under cover.

"Now," said Nicholas, mopping his brow, "the word is—tea! Though first, Bill, can you tell me why the markets are so consistently bad?"

"Ay, sir, 'tis because our cattle, though fairish, can't nowise compare wi' the best, and only the best goes in Sussex. And what wi' Lord Windover's prime stock and t'other rich farmers yereabouts, ourn don't do. When Miss Jo's feyther were alive, ah, them were the grand days, our beasts was famous; but since he died, mistus have been that poor as she can't buy the best to breed from, so our stock don't fetch top prices nowadays—it aren't to be ax-pected, which be doleful!"

"Yet which gives me an idea, Bill."

"May I ax ee wot, sir?"

"An idea best described by the word 'splendorious'. Yes, by George and the Dragon, Bill, so much so that instead of quaffing Bohea or sipping Souchong, I'll go and set about it pronto, which means 'now'!"

CHAPTER XXI

How the "Splendorious" Idea Inspired Action

IMPELLED by this sudden idea, Nicholas took his way by field-path and bowery lane until before him rose the chimneys and gables of that smallish, cosy homestead called Willowbrook, and great was his surprise and pleasure to see this erstwhile lonely and desolate house had wakened to new and joyous life, its plaster and timbering freshly white-washed and painted, its once blank lattices, now daintily curtained, glowed and glittered in the westering sunlight, its gates mended, the weeds of its garden were banished, its chimneys smoked, while from the yard beyond a cow lowed and a man whistled cheerily above the sound of hammer and saw plied with equal vigour.

So thither strode Nicholas where the two sailor brethren were hard at work.

"Well now, love me eyes!" exclaimed Ben, sitting by his hammer. "We'm main glad to see you, sir—eh, Bob?"

"Ay ay, Ben, and heartily!" answered Brother Bob, loosing his saw. Thus they hailed and greeted each other like the old shipmates they were.

"Sir," quoth Bob, "my Soo and her sister Poll have stood away to Horsham shopping, but if your honour will honour us, in a drop or so o' grog now——"

"No thanks, Bob, I'm here on business—but first I must congratulate you on how wonderfully you have improved the old place, and so speedily, too!"

"Ay, sir, we'm getting her shipshape, Brother Ben and me; ah, and my Soo has fell in love wi' the house sir, inboard and out, from trucks to keelson, and so has Sister Poll, eh Ben?"

"Ay, both on 'em abrushing of her and ascrubbing of her alow and aloft while Bob and me scours and paints her, fore and aft—eh, Brother Bob?"

"Ay, she'll be a picture, Mr. Anson, when we've done to her all as us do mean for to do—eh, Ben?"

"Ay, she'll be right smart, sir, and all ataunto afore long."

"What stock have you, Bob, cows and so on?"

"Well, sir, we'm beginning very cautious—eh, Ben?"

"None was ever cautiouser, sir."

"So, Mr. Anson, we'm commencing with one horse, a brace o' cows in milk, a dozen cocks and hens as be mostly cocks, four sheep and a sow doo to farrow at any minute—eh, Ben?"

"Ay, sir, us be ex-pecting—constant! So I'm keeping my weather eye on her con-tinual."

"So you see, sir, we ain't pre-cisely over-stocked, as yet."

"Consequently, Bob, you have plenty of room for such cattle as I wish you to buy for me."

"With j'y, sir. But are you turning farmer likewise?"

"Well, no, Bob, it's a scheme that occurred to me . . . harkee, old shipmates!"

So now, seating himself on upturned bucket, Nicholas expounded his splendorious idea while these sailor brethren, perched together on a shaft of their one and only wagon, listened mutely and in ever-growing wonder, though neither uttered a word until Nicholas had made an end.

"So, Mr. Anson, your orders is for us to be at every sale and to beat every bid, no matter how high?"

"Sky-high, Bob; the higher you buy, the better I shall be pleased! You will buy all and any Fallowdene cattle and at my price! Sheep or lambs, calves, bullocks or cows —whatever prices are offered you will double them and buy."

"But, sir, that'll come mighty expensive, won't it?"

"I hope so, old shipmate. The more you pay the better I shall be pleased!"

"Well now, sir, drowned me if I ain't all took aback and ashivering in the wind's eye—eh, Ben?"

"Ay, sir, you have brought us up wi' a round turn— eh, Bob?"

"That you have, sir! For wherefore buy dear instead o' cheap? Sir, I'm all adrift and don't fathom your meaning."

"You will, Bob, when I tell you there is a lady in the case."

"Oh? Ah! Then, sir, we do—eh, Ben?"

"Ay, sir, heartily!"

"Well now, my hearties," said Nicholas, rising, "since this is now perfectly understood, I make this further proposal to you; the cattle you buy for me at my price you shall buy from me at their true market price and in your own time. Is this also understood?"

"Ay, Mr. Anson, sir, and it don't seem neither right nor fair to yourself—eh, Ben?"

"No, Bob, it don't and therefore can't be, sir. Our gain would be your loss, sir, wherefore Bob and me can't, don't, and won't agree thereto."

"However," said Nicholas, laying a hand on the shoulder of each, "good friends and shipmates, this is my wish, my will and most strict command, so—how about it—you, Bob?"

"Why, Mr. Anson, orders now as ever, being orders, all as I can say is ay ay and mightily grateful——"

"And you, Ben?"

"I says—same as Bob, your honour, adding the word rum, sir! Grog to show somewhat of our gratitood—eh, Bob?"

"Ay ay, brother, grog it is!"

Thus the western sky was aflame with sunset as Nicholas wended villagewards, feeling at peace with all the world and dreaming of a happy future—which, of course, meant Joanne. Wherefore the better to meditate upon this most precious subject, he paused beside a certain stile to lean there and gaze upon that western glory the while he set his thought into rhyme, thus:

> "Oh Mistress Mine, of beauty rare,
>   With sunset tangled in thy hair,
>   This should my light and beacon be,
>   Through every shoal safe-guiding me,
>   Through death itself, until——"

Here indeed Death, it seemed, smote at him, so that he would have fallen but for the stile whereto he clung instinctively, being for the moment blinded, half-stunned and perfectly helpless.

"Turn! And show your cursed face!" cried a voice behind him. "Turn and take the thrashing you deserve! Turn and face me!" Mutely Nicholas obeyed, supported by the stile, and leaned thus until, his vision clearing, he beheld Lord Wolverton uncoiling the lash of his whip to draw it through his fingers caressingly.

"Aha, bumpkin," he said, chuckling with ferocious glee, "that rap on your loutish nob was merely a beginning! I'm going to lash you, bumpkin, for your persistent insolence; ha yes, I'm going to thrash you until I'm tired or you howl and whine for mercy—d'ye hear? D'ye see this horse-whip?"

"Yes!" muttered Nicholas.

"Then—feel it!" The whip was raised, Nicholas lifted feeble arms to shield his face as the long lash cracked viciously, hissed and stung him so cruelly that he flinched.

"So—ho!" laughed his tormentor. "You certainly felt that, eh, my impudent yokel, eh? Hurt you, didn't it?"

"Yes!" said Nicholas.

"Ah well, I'm enjoying myself immensely, so there'll be plenty more, like—this!"

Again that merciless whip cracked, and again Nicholas cowered and flinched to the sharp-biting lash . . . But then, his faintness passing, he leapt to action at last; and never in his many encounters afloat and ashore had he plied fists so joyfully or to such devastating effect. My lord's whip flew one way, his hat another, and himself, reeling from hard-driving left, followed by bone-jarring right, spun round and staggered backwards until checked painfully by the stile. . . . Thus it was my lord who now hung there dazed and helpless, nor moved he until, powerful hands clutching him by the collar, he was lifted and shaken with sickening violence. But, as he stared up at the grim face so near his own, he contrived to gasp his amazement:

"Harbourne! By heavens . . . you're . . . Harbourne!"

"Yes!" said Nicholas for the third time; then, loosing his hold, dropped Lord Wolverton, who, sprawling in the dust, made no effort to rise. "Yes," said Nicholas again, and rather breathlessly, "I'm Harbourne, and what now?" Whereto, and more breathlessly, my lord made answer:

"Now I . . . ap-pologise . . . for the . . . damn whip. . . . So . . . let me be."

"Why the devil should I . . . cut short my pleasure, for now I'm enjoying myself . . . and without a whip!"

"Because you've . . . done enough, and I've . . . had . . . more than enough . . . half throttled . . . besides my damaged nose and lip. . . ."

"However, my lord, I fancy a little more would do us both good——"

"And I'm . . . perfectly certain it . . . would not! And Sir Nicholas Harbourne couldn't . . . strike a man when he's down, surely?"

"No, but he might kick a Wolverton until he stands up——"

"Never! I'm down and down I shall remain and . . . defy your brutality from the accursed dust of my abasement . . . once again craving pardon for . . . the whip. But how the devil could I know you for Sir Nicholas with your damn countryman's lingo and get-up . . . hobnails and so on? You took me in completely . . . though why you should so deceive Joanne is beyond comprehension."

The whip, that instrument of torture, chancing to lie near, Nicholas took it up and, in his turn, caressed the cruel lash, saying:

"Wolverton, I object strongly to your word 'deceive'!"

"Then, Sir Nicholas, I retract it instantly! I withdraw the expression and beg you to forget it."

Nicholas cracked the whip like a pistol-shot, sighed regretfully, and tossed it into the ditch.

"Sir," said he rather mournfully, shaking his head at Lord Wolverton who was now seated cross-legged in the dust, "your abjection disarms me! Unhappily I cannot whip you in cold blood any more than I could a baby. All that remains is for me to take leave of you and, once more for good—I hope!"

"Spoken, Harbourne, like the gentleman you are."

"But this evening, sir, I repeat—we part for good and all. I cannot hope or expect you will not betray my identity to Miss Joanne, soon or late—but, my lord, should I find you on my land or anywhere near Fallowdene, if ever I do, then by all I hold sacred in life I'll fit you for a hospital bed."

"You've done that already!" sighed my lord, glancing down at his torn coat made pinker now by divers spots and darker stains from his battered features. "But I utter no complaint, Harbourne. I esteem myself fortunate to be no worse than I am—considering the whip. Rest assured, I shall keep well out of your reach henceforth, though I shall keep you well in mind!"

"My lord, I don't doubt it, or that you will seek to

harm me, at your leisure and when I least expect it, if you can do so without risk to your precious self, of course."

"Harbourne, I find it painful to laugh or even smile, with a split lip, at your natural fearful suspicions! Instead, by your kind permission I will rise and seek my horse yonder and we will go our appointed ways—you to supper and a cosy bed, I to a surgeon and bandages. So in bidding you be content with your handiwork, Harbourne, I also bid you good evening and—goodbye!"

So they parted, and thus Nicholas thought no more of versifying, at least for the present.

CHAPTER XXII

The Wherefore of Bill's Black Eye

DURING the latter days of this golden August Nicholas, having finished the pigsties to general admiration and more or less his own finical satisfaction, now set himself to learn all he might by word and example of his very able fellow-labourers, the Faithful Three: from solemn George the use of a bill-hook and the true art of 'laying' a hedge; from hearty, ever-ready Bill the manage of swap-hook or sickle and that more subtle implement, the scythe; from cheery old Joe the divers moods and proper manipulation "o' they pesky critters, cows", and how in their milking "each on 'em, bein' fee-male, and therefore con-trairy like, each must be 'andled different to make 'em give copious and free".

Today Nicholas, bare of arm and throat, was scything grass in the paddock for practice, and so profoundly intent on each long smooth stroke of the keen blade, as to be totally unaware of the lovely eyes that watched his every movement; also Joanne had taken care to approach un-heard. So now as she gazed at his intent face and lithely powerful frame, she questioned herself regarding him, on this wise:

Was he handsome? No! With that relentless line of mouth, aggressive jut of chin and deep-set eyes—most certainly not! Yet to be sure he looked—comfortably strong. Those bronzed arms, for instance, though vulgarly brawny and brutally compelling, could be unexpectedly gentle and immensely restful—to such fast young women, abandoned creatures, who enjoyed being hugged and grappled in manner so odiously bearlike. However, nobody could think him a handsome man—with that craggy chin and beak of a nose. . . . Yet his mouth, when not grim-set, was shapely enough—in a way. As for his eyes, grey and black-lashed, these were his best feature undoubtedly, for they could be very eloquent and look at her with expression of such—they were indeed—yes, these eyes were looking at her now with expression of most rapturous surprise as, and with mouth at its shapeliest, he murmured:

"Oh Lady of the Sunlight, thou Spirit of this Glad Summer, I humbly thank God for the sight of thee!"

Then with scythe in one hand and hat in the other, he bowed reverently, saying thereafter and more lightly: "Oh—mistress mine, God give thee as much joy of this fair, sweet morn!"

For a moment she stood hushed and still, returning his gaze with one as eloquent—almost; then:

"Kind and gentle sir, I thank you!" she replied, and sank before him in profound and graceful curtsy. "In faith and good sooth," she laughed, "I do think Old Sol up yonder hath touched us with his magic, some spell o' wizendry! For truly I am very joyful, Anthony. But who wouldn't be, with that same dear old sun beaming on us so kindly and with promise of a grand and wonderful harvest? Look yonder, there's glory for you!" and she gestured towards where the wide cornfields stretched away in yellowing splendour. "Oh," she sighed happily, "it will be, it must be, a rich, most bounteous harvest! Unless . . . all I fear now is the future . . . storm and tempest, wind and rain——"

"Now why," he demanded, "Lord love you, Joanne, why on earth worry before you need? Why be so terrified of the future?"

"Because, since my dear capable father died, the future, for me at least, has held so very much of fearful anxiety that worry has become a habit—which is very silly of me, I suppose. Yes, and especially now that our cattle are selling so marvellously well at last—so amazingly well that today, after tea, I—and Aunt Jemima, of course—can repay your kind loan, every farthing, with our grateful thanks and my infinite relief."

"Oh? And pray why such immense relief?"

"Because I cannot bear to owe anything to anyone and most especially—to our handyman! Which is laudable and very natural, isn't it?"

"No!" he answered (mouth grim and chin craggy). "It's absurdly preposterous!"

"Oh, is it indeed?" she demanded in sudden, angry defiance.

"Yes, indeed it is, and also perfectly ridiculous!"

"Please," said she, as suddenly meek, "please may I be allowed to ask why?"

"Because," he replied (mouth shapely again), "your handyman, being Anthony, is so completely yours—if you will only take the poor fellow."

"Why should I?" she murmured.

"To make for him the home he dreams about and longs

for, that sacred place that only you can or ever shall make."

"Why—only me?" And never had her voice been so gentle or her look so tender as she waited his reply—the right, the proper and only answer . . .

"Because," said he, "you and I were meant for one anoth——"

"Oh!" she exclaimed, with voice and tone neither tender nor gentle since she had instantly transformed herself into a young fury. "Oh—get on with your hateful scything—do!"

"Eh . . . oh . . . I will!" said he, utterly confounded. "But why the adjective 'hateful'?"

"Because!" she retorted scornfully.

"Because—what, pray?"

"Fool!" she retorted, and away she sped, leaving him to marvel at her bewildering change of mood and the vagaries of women in general. Still pondering this problem, he had paused to resharpen his scythe, when to him came Bill, dusty of person and with a black eye, to which last he drew attention by saying:

"Tom Turner give me this yere heye, sir!"

"Oh? Well, I've seen blacker, old fellow——"

"Ar, but, sir, you should ought to see what I give Tom Turner! Two on 'em, sir, ar, both on 'em, and I likewise drawed 'is claret proper."

"Bravo, old lad! But who is Tom Turner, and why the violence?"

"Tom be Lord Wolverton's chief drover, sir, and I threshed him for speakin' disrespectful of our Mistus Joanne."

"Then bravo again, Bill! What did the damn rascal dare to say?"

"Sir, 'twere summat as I couldn't abide nor let pass. 'Twere summat out-rageous! Ar, and arl b'reason o' summat else as has been a-puzzlin' o' me frequent."

"What, Bill? Let's hear."

"Our cattle, sir! They've been toppin' the market— constant!"

"Well, so much the better!"

"No, sir, axing your pardin, 'tis so much the worse, for they've been sellin' at better prices than them as was better stock!"

"But surely, Bill, that's all to the good?"

"No again, sir, it be arl to the bad. For at they markets be farmers and dealers as knows the true worth of every breed o' cattle—and seein' as ourn is bought constant at prices far beyond their proper worth, it set folk atalkin', then alaughin', then nudging each other and whisperin' and—well—that's the reason as I've got this yere eye."

"Bill, I'm afraid I don't understand."

"Sir, last evenin' I'm in the Black Hoss taking a pint, when in come Turner along of others, and, seein' me, he laughs and, says 'e, 'Ho Bill,' 'e says, 'has him as buys arl your beasts at sich fool prices bought your Mistus Joanne along of em?' 'e says——"

"Oh, curse the fellow!"

"I did, sir, very 'earty! I likewise throwed my ale in his face——"

"Good! I hope you drubbed him well."

"Mist' Anthony, I did, no question! I stopped 'is mouth wi' both my fist-ees, one arter t'other; I likewise

M

filled up both his eyes. But, sir, there's plenty other mouths and tongues to wag, as I can't stop nohow, which be doleful!"

"Damnation!" exclaimed Nicholas. "What a devilish, evil-thinking world this is!"

"So it be, sir, sure-ly! But wot I'd like to know is— who are these fools as bid and buy our cattle so out-rageous high to blacken and dishonour the good name of our mistus? . . . Lordy-lord, yere she comes and 'er must never see this yere eye o' mine in mourning——"

"Then get behind this tree, quick, man!"

With a leap Bill did so, yet not speedily enough to escape those bright eyes, for as Joanne drew near she called, gaily:

"Oh, Bill, why have you tried to vanish? Are you and Mr. Anthony playing hide and seek? Why cower behind this tree which is too small to hide you—so come out and tell me. My gracious! What have you been doing to yourself?"

"Nary a thing, Miss Jo."

"But your poor eye! Whatever happened?"

"Eh, marm? Eye, Miss Jo?"

"Yes, eye! Your left one. No, don't slink or try to steal away. Tell me how it happened."

"A bit of a accident, Miss Jo."

"Lift your head and let me look at it. Ah, as I thought! Bill, this accident was someone's brutal fist! Not Mr. Anthony's, I hope?"

"Lorramitey—no, mistus—no sich thing!"

"But you have been fighting someone."

" 'Twere only a bit of a go, Miss Jo."

"Then you've been drinking also!"

"Only a pint or so——"

"Not with Mr. Anthony, I trust?"

"No, marm! Him and me hasn't drank a spot together since the day as you met 'im along o' me at the Peck o'——"

"However, I'm afraid Mr. Anthony has a bad influence upon you—being himself so fond of ale and a much too-ready fighter!"

"Marm and mistus," said Anthony, speaking at last and in his best Sussexese, "theer do be times when it be a man's dooty for to fight, and my friend Bill done 'is dooty noble, ar, very 'andsome and proper, like the man 'e be."

"All fighting is brutal!" she retorted. "And all brutality is hatefully wrong."

"Yes, of course it is!" he admitted. "But unhappily, just as 'of course' it is a necessary evil and must be until aggressive brutality is tamed. Where would our Old England be without such sturdy men as Bill to fight for her, ay, and Civilisation, too! Answer me that, marm, if so be ee can!"

"Not while this 'sturdy' victim of Brutality needs my attention. Come along, Bill, that eye shall be bathed——"

"Thankee, Miss Jo, but I'd rayther not."

"Indoors, you disobedient, fighting, violent wretch—come along!" And, meekly submissive, he obeyed. Nicholas, leaning on the shaft of his scythe, watched until they were out of sight, then he smiled, sighed and bent again to his labour; thus he had mowed a wideish area when back came Bill very self-consciously, because of the neat white bandage that swathed "the eye", whereon his weatherbeaten old hat was perched at jaunty angle.

"So—ho!" laughed Nicholas. "She's put your eye in a sling, eh, Bill?"

"Ar, sir, and wi' a cold-water pad onto it! But 'twixt you and me, I can do and see a sight better without un, so I'll tak' it off. Mistus Jo likewise bathed it, then 'intment, and she done it arl so gentle and tender like as 'twere a angel o' marcy!"

"Ay," said Nicholas, voicing his thought on impulse. "She can be gentle as any holy angel—though with the devil of a temper."

"But only because she needs marrying, sir."

"Eh? Oh! D'ye think so, Bill?"

"Ar, no question, sir—though a man o' the right sort, o' course."

"What sort would be the right sort, Bill?"

"Well, sir, if I may mak' s' bold, I'd say—one o' your sort, Mist' Anthony."

"Old fellow, I agree with you so heartily that should you chance anywhere near the Soaring Lark this evening, say, we will quaff a flagon together."

"Sir, ee do me proud, ar, by goles ee do, sir, for not long ago you called me—your friend."

"So you are, yes, and one I esteem as the right kind of Englishman, than whom there are none better! For we are of the breed that taught mankind the blessedness of freedom to think and act and——"

Faint and far beyond those yellowing cornfields came that gladly familiar cry:

"An—toe—nee!"

"And there," said Bill, glancing thitherward, "there comes another angel, sir, which, being younger, is nigher to heaven, I rackon!"

"True, Bill! You love her also, eh?"

"Ar, ever since she were born, sir."

"Have you no family, no children of your own, old fellow?"

"No, sir, and never shall 'ave, because . . . she as might have give 'em to me . . . died premmytoor and there'll never be no other. She were nursemaid to Miss Jo —and that's why, Miss Jo or no—I shall never leave Fallerdene . . . for she worked here along o' me . . . belonged here, same as me and does so still! Sometimes I seems to 'ear 'er futsteps, quick and light, coming to meet me like she did years ago when I were foldin' the sheep or herding the cattle. Ar, though she be dead these ten years and more. . . . She lives in my mind and allus will—so long as I can think, if you twig my meaning, Mist' Anthony."

"I do, Bill, yes—I do! Memory can be a blessedness and——"

"An—toe—nee!"

With hair and sunbonnet flying behind her as usual, Priscilla came speeding—to be caught up, kissed and throned upon her Anthony's shoulder, all quite as usual, though now she enquired:

"Why did Bill go so quick, without saying good afternoon, or how-do-I-do, or anything?"

"Perhaps because he saw you were—quite well, thank you."

"Oh, I see! Well, tonight, my Anthony, it's his-tree again, all about burning martyrs and those poor bishops named Riddle and Crammer and how when they were chained to the stake they talked of lighting a candle and I don't know why when they were all alight, so what do you s'pose they meant?"

"That by dying, sweetheart, and dying so very bravely for their belief, they were lighting a flame in people's hearts, far brighter and greater than the fire that burned their poor bodies—a flame that has never gone out and never will."

CHAPTER XXIII

Harvest

" 'COME, ye thankful people, come!' "

High and sweetly clear Priscilla was singing amid the golden sheaves, for it was harvest-time, and she, like the small presiding genius of this glad festival, sang thus until the many reapers, who had come from near and far, men, women and children, took up the refrain in happy chorus as they wrought, cutting, gathering and binding into sheaves this splendid, heavy-headed corn while the children and elder women gleaned such of the precious grain as fell by the way.

"Come ee, Mist' Anthony, come ee now 'long o' we," piped old Joe. "Leave that ork'ard scythe and tek this extry swap-'ook and do as me, lookee! I teks me an 'ole armful o' corn—so, then,"—with one dexterous stroke of sickle he cut through the many stalks—"and theer she be, a sheaf layin' ready for the binders."

Hour after hour scythe and sickle-blades gleamed and glittered while from a cloudless heaven the sun beamed as if to bless their labour, though:

"Perishin' 'ot it be!" said old Joe at last.

"Ar!" quoth stolid George, pausing to set a new edge to his blade. "But no man never see no better corn than ourn, eh, Bill?"

"Never, Jarge! And no when!"

"However," sighed Nicholas, mopping brow on brawny forearm, "Joe's right—it is infernally hot!" Here scythes and sickles gleamed in action again, and no word spoken until:

"I rackon," said old Joe, straightening his back, "this yere right no-bel crop'll mean fortun' to Mistus Joanne."

"And j'y!" quoth George.

"Ar, if only the weather bides fair!" quoth Bill.

"Well, and wherefore shouldn't it?" demanded Joe.

"Old un, I didn't nowise like the sunset yesterday, nor yet the look o' the moon!"

"You be too fancy-free in the 'ead, Bill me lad, too i-magination-a-tive, you be!"

"And you, Joe, don't 'ave no ideas at all, beyond the udder of a cow! And, wot's more——"

But at this moment came Ann, to curtsy demurely to Nicholas, smile askance at conscious George, and, Hebe-like, proffer them choice of cool cider or small beer. . . . Thus, happily refreshed and invigorated, they fell to work again, all heedless of the sun glare. But as the day wore on, Bill paused oftener to glance anxiously across green and bowery landscape to that far sheen that was the sea. At last, Nicholas remarking on this, he answered:

"Sir, there was too much red i' the sunset last evening and later a ring about the moon."

"Bad weather coming, eh, Bill?"

"Ar, so I fear, sir!"

"Though it looks fair enough at present, old fellow."

"So it do, sir, sure-ly! Howsever, we uns all had better work our best as us may."

So, work indeed they did, all four, and Nicholas so intent that, after some while, starting to a touch, he glanced up to see Bill pointing where up from that distant sea a cloud was rising, small as yet but ominous.

"Is that what you feared, Bill?"

"And it be acomin', sir! The word for arl on us now is 'speed'—a race agin' yon threat o' tempest! I'll go warn our reapers every man and——" But, even as he spoke, towards them came Joanne, light of foot, flushed of cheek, bright of eye, all radiant with splendid, vigorous life and the abounding joy of it.

"Well," she cried gaily, "my faithful three—I mean four—what a grand harvest and, oh, what a glorious day for it! And, goodness me, how furiously you are all working! Why such quite astonishing haste—and in this heat?"

And without pausing in his labour, Bill replied:

"Seawards, Miss Jo! Look seawards—there be your answer and the reason for our fur'ous speed, which be doleful!"

"Only a cloud, Bill, and very small!"

"Ar, but 'twill grow—and grow—big wi' rageful storm——"

"Oh!" she gasped, clasping her hands. "Oh, Bill, do you think so?"

"Marm, I dread so! 'Twill be a race 'twixt us reapers and yon tempest as be acoming——"

"God forbid!" she exclaimed, gazing very fearfully now at that ominous cloud. "If you are right it will mean—ruin——"

"Ar, doleful!"

"So I hope and pray you are mistaken, Bill."

"So do I, Miss Jo, wi' arl my 'eart!"

"And I think you are wrong; that cloud doesn't seem to be growing . . . and yet . . . it looks . . . rather awful."

" 'Owsever, Miss Jo, 'tis best as ee d'go and warn arl the folk to work right speedy, for fear."

"Yes, ah, yes, I will!" she cried, and sped away. . . .

Thus, scythe and sickle blades were plied now faster than ever before, in desperate endeavour to save this bounteous harvest, or as much of it as possible; for as the afternoon sun began to decline and sink westward, the cloud rose ever higher, spread ever wider, grew ever blacker; and the corn was mowed, bound into sheaves and carted to safety until, as they laboured thus without stay or respite, above them loomed this dreadful blackness putting out the kindly sun, and in this denser gloom an icy breath, a vague stirring, a sudden gust with spatter of driven rain followed by the sullen growl of distant thunder and growing riot of wind. . . . Then, high and clear above this waxing tumult, Joanne's voice:

"Come now, everybody . . . we have done all we can and—God knows I'm grateful to you all. . . . But you can do no more. . . . So now into the great barn for tea . . . every one of you, come." Scarcely had they reached this welcome haven than the tempest smote in wildest fury with rush and roar of a mighty wind and lash of hissing rain.

"Sir," said Bill, close beside Nicholas, "us 'ave saved pretty much o' the crop, I rackon, but for the rest is doleful ruination! Ay, but our Mistus Joanne do take her gurt loss right valiant—will ee just look at her!"

"I am, Bill; I am, of course. God bless her! Handing out cake and cups of tea, and, oh bless her again, smiling!"

"Our Miss Jo be a right, great-'earted creeter, sir, no question!"

"Ay, no question, Bill, and truly noble lady." For indeed while this storm raged above and around them, working ruin upon her crops and all hope of the richly bounteous harvest that would have been, Joanne, hiding her grievous disappointment, played her part of smiling hostess, going to and fro among the reapers, quick to see and minister to their wants; and when the thunder rolled near to blind them with vivid lightning flash and deafen them with earth-shaking crash, it was she who spoke so cheerfully to the fearful children and clasped the terrified in the soothing comfort of her arms.

"And there, Mist' Anthony," quoth Bill, as the storm's wild fury abated, "there is a wife as could lift a man above himself, I rackon, ar, and up to the footstool o' God at last!"

"Old fellow," said Nicholas, "is any man truly worthy of such a wife? No, not one, and least of all—such as I!" So saying, moved by sudden impulse, he stepped out from the barn and, heedless of the rain which was lessening, came where he could behold the pitiful waste and devastation of those once glorious fields.

"Hi—you there!"

Glancing round, Nicholas beheld a rain-sodden horseman, a stranger who enquired for "Miss Joanne".

"Who wants her?" demanded Nicholas.

"Me, for sure!"

"And who the devil are you?"

"A messenger. Got a letter for her, I have."

"Who from?"

"My master Lord Wolverton."

"Very well, give it to me and I'll——"

"Oh no! I'm to give it to none but herself!"

"So? Then be damned!" And away strode Nicholas, scowling, since he guessed what that letter portended; and now his thought was:

"Why the devil didn't I whip him?"

But presently this was banished by a sweeter, far lovelier thought—of Joanne rising above her own distress to comfort others; and, remembering his question, 'Is any man worthy such a wife?' he answered himself again and aloud:

"No, not one, and least of all I!"

In this mood of most unusual humility, Nicholas wended villagewards, because now to his love was added a profound awe for the unselfish, valiant heart of her who, at this precise moment, was lying face down upon her bed, weeping in very passion of grief—not for the ruined harvest, no—her heart, it seemed, was breaking because of disillusion and the letter that lay crumpled beside her tear-wet pillow.

CHAPTER XXIV

Describes a Hate-filled Letter

IT WAS next morning; Priscilla had just departed (unwillingly) to school, and now Aunt Jemima, seated at one side of the table, seemed busied with a smallish, neat volume labelled: Household Accounts, while Joanne, sitting directly opposite, was gazing down, head in hands, at a closely written, extremely crumpled sheet of paper which her aunt, screened as it were behind Household Accounts, had contrived to see began with the words, penned in familiar scrawl, "My poor, deluded Joanne".

Wherefore, after some while, Aunt Jemima spoke, serenely gentle as usual:

"Your letter, I think, is from your Lord Wolverton, poor fellow!"

"He is not mine—yet! And why the 'poor fellow', Aunt?"

"I met Doctor Stacey in the village yesterday who informed me he had been attending his lordship for cuts and bruises and general shock, the result of an accident— thrown from his horse, I fancy. Are you listening, my dear?" she enquired, for Joanne was staring down at the letter again.

"Yes—yes, of course I am, and it serves him exactly

right for being so reckless! And he always uses his spurs too much."

"Oh, but, my dear—he looks so splendid on horseback; you told me so, and I'm sure——"

Joanne actually and positively snorted; Aunt Jemima smiled behind Household Accounts and so was silence, until:

"My dear, by the way you are frowning—quite a scowl! —I infer your love letter cannot——"

"Oh, for mercy's sake, hush, Aunt, and let me read. And it is—not a love letter! Now do be quiet!"

"Oh, my sweet pet, I will be silent as a mouse."

"Mice aren't silent! And please forgive me for snapping at you."

"Certainly, child, because I think you were really snapping at your letter, or its writer—were you?"

"No—yes. Oh, I don't know!"

Nor did she, for the letter she had read so often and with such varying emotions was this:

"My poor, deluded Joanne,

"As one to whom you are very dear, even to marriage, which I now offer you again, I feel it my bounden duty to warn you against the double-faced rascal who, to save himself from exposure of what he truly is, very nearly murdered me lately upon the road. Yes, my dear deceived Joanne, this same rogue who, under a false name, masquerades as your humble farm labourer, this liar who has inflicted himself upon you so insidiously and may try to win the innocent confidence of yourself and Aunt, is in reality a thief, a self-confessed cheat and card-sharper whom I unmasked and denounced and threatened with expulsion from the clubs and honourable society after he had tricked me out of a considerable sum of money.

"And this scoundrel's true name is Harbourne, a fellow most unworthy the title and such vast wealth, which by some jugglery of fate he now bears. It is in evidence that he was of such evil character, his uncle, Sir Jonas, cast him off, and thus his detested nephew Nicholas became a world rover and ruffian knock-about sailor, living as best he could by sheer brutality at sea or cunning trickery on land, as he confessed to me. Such is the villain who, lifted by blind Destiny from deeps of depravity to wealth and title, now makes pretence to be the gentleman and man of honour he is not, never was, and never can be. Lastly, you must know, my dear, proud Joanne, he has made of your fair name a laughing-stock—yes, and worse, in every market lately, in buying, through his agents, all your cattle at prices so absurdly above their proper value that now it is whispered that some wealthy unknown is thus buying, or has bought, you also. Thus I have opened your lovely eyes to these facts; it is for you to prove them, challenge him, question him and, seeing his guilt, know them for truth and myself,

"Your ever devoted,

"CHARLES, LORD WOLVERTON.

"P.S. You may show him this letter, and should he then desire a gentlemanly meeting, I will honour him by exchanging shots on Calais Sands whenever he chooses to die."

And it was at this postscript Joanne was gazing as her aunt, smiling behind Household Accounts, enquired:

"May I be privileged to see that letter, my dear?"

"Yes—no! No, not now. Ah, but you shall, my dear, comforting angel-aunt." Then, folding the letter very carefully, Joanne arose, put on her shady sun-bonnet and went forth to seek, find and challenge this basest of deceivers, Sir Nicholas Harbourne.

CHAPTER XXV

Tells How She Asked Questions and He Tried to Answer

SHE CONFRONTED him by the pigsties on his way to the devastated cornfields, and Nicholas, warned by her look and the letter in her clenched hand, braced himself for the expected furious tirade; but when she spoke it was in tone almost casual:

"If you can possibly speak the truth, do so now and tell me your real name." And, returning her searching gaze with one as steadfast, he answered, gesturing carelessly towards that very crumpled letter:

"Surely Wolverton has informed you that I am Nicholas Harbourne, but I am also Anthony Anson, humbly and for ever yours to serve and——"

"Did you win a great sum of money from my lord, and—by cheating?"

"I did indeed, and it was a pleasure beyond my expec——"

"Is that how you—possessed yourself of my father's promissory note?"

"Yes—in a way. For when I had cleaned out Wolverton quite completely, I——"

"You mean by cheating him—to his ruin?"

"Absolutely and most thoroughly! Then, using his own money I compelled——"

"Did my lord discover your hateful trickery and force you to confess?"

"Your lord did not! Quite the reverse, he wailed and——"

"Didn't he threaten you——"

"Wildly and wailfully, but to no purp——"

"Threaten to denounce you publicly for a shameful cheat, a—thief?"

"Yes, he was very amusing——"

"Amusing?" she cried. "To be threatened with exposure, expelled ignominiously from all the clubs and honourable society—do you dare call that 'amusing'?"

"Yes, Joanne, it is extremely laughable considering—considering my accuser is, as I say, sus——"

"Don't! You've said enough—too much—Sir Nicholas!"

"But, Joanne," he sighed reproachfully though with the merriest twinkle in his eyes, "how can I when you interrupt me continually? Now if you will allow me to tell you how the 'biter was bit', we'll laugh together and——"

"Laugh?" she repeated. "And about such hateful wickedness?"

"Neither wicked nor hateful, Joanne, but delightfully funny! Yes, by Saint George and his confounded Dragon, so comical that I——"

"Oh!" she gasped, recoiling in horrified dismay. "Are you so utterly beyond all sense of guilt or feeling of shame?"

"I am indeed!" he nodded, and actually laughed. "I soar above all such, on pinions of probity and triumphant achievement! For, oh, mistress mine——"

"No!" she cried passionately. "I will not permit——
You shall never call me so again, never! I forbid it."

"Never is quite a time, Joanne. Sometimes it means a
whole livelong day. Sometimes even a week! And so
I——"

"Oh!" she cried again with wild, despairing gesture.
"No wonder you are such a—a brutal fighter! Your
dreadfully wickedly horrible past life has so warped—so
debased you that I don't know how to talk with detestably mocking Sir Nicholas Harbourne."

"Then please don't try. Instead of constantly inter-
rupting, permit your humble handyman, your poor, meek
Anthony a word or so of explanation and he——"

"Yes!" she cried and now in hot fury. "Oh yes I will!
He—you—shall explain your cruel, shameful treatment of
me—— No! First I will hear more of hatefully con-
temptible Sir Nicholas Harbourne, the odious, smiling,
hypocritical deceiver, the two-faced cunning beast
and——"

"Now, Joanne, for mercy's sake, pause and take a deep,
deep breath!"

"Oh, you may laugh and mock because, thanks to my
lord, I know you at last for what you truly are, so answer
and admit this for truth. When your Uncle Jonas, for
your wickedness, cast you off, you were very poor?"

"I was destitute, Joanne, but——"

"Did you then become a vagabond and—thief?"

"Oh no, merely a cabin-boy aboard a ship outward
bound for——"

"Later on, did you live by every kind of cheating and
trickery?"

"Not every kind. No, I devoted my energies to cards and known crooked gamblers. I swallowed such land-sharks whole and lived very well on them and by them. Come now, if you will hear more of my black and hideous past, let us sit down together—here in the pigsty and——"

"Sir Nicholas, before we part, I demand to know why you have so bitterly defamed me——"

"God forbid!" he exclaimed, and with the utmost fervour, though she continued as if he had not spoken:

"Why have you made my name a byword in the county, a—shameful laughing stock? Today I am deemed a vile creature to be—bought like my cattle! Oh—horrible!"

"Joanne!" he sighed with tone and look of deepest remorse, reaching out both hands imploringly.

"No!" she cried, shrinking from him. "Ah—don't touch me! Go—go and never come back! I despise you, hate you and always shall, your voice, your looks—all of you, and never want to see or hear you again!"

And so—away she sped in such blind fury of grief, anger and despair that once she stumbled and nearly fell; but, reaching the house and the mute comfort of Aunt Jemima's gentle presence, she cried and in tone almost gleeful:

"I've got rid of him, Aunt! Yes, I've rid myself of the vile, deceitful wretch. Now read this letter and you will know why." Then, tossing this much-crumpled missive upon the table, she crossed the spacious sitting-room, opened the door and vanished with sound extremely sob-like.

Aunt Jemima, serene as ever, smoothed the wrinkled paper and began to read . . .

Meanwhile Nicholas stood in dismayed perplexity scowling at the row of pigsties, nor moved until out from behind them stepped Bill, as greatly dismayed and no less perplexed:

"Sir," said he apologetically, "me chancin' for to be where I were, accidental like, and no chance to go anywhere else without Miss Jo ketchin' sight o' me, I bided where I were and so I couldn't nowise 'elp but over'ear arl as took place, every word. And so, sir, I be so shook as I dunno wot—first b'reason as she's give ee notice for to quit, and second, seein' 'as 'ow you—'stead o' being the man as could work so praper and j'yful along o' we and ply 'ammer, saw and scythe so 'andsome—ain't that man, none wotever, seeing as 'ow you be oo you be and, so being, being yourself real and true, be a gen'leman and one o' the Quality."

"Nonsense, Bill! I am that same man, now as ever, and well you know it, damn it!"

"Axing your pardin, sir, but you ain't and cannot nowise be not nohow, seein' as 'ow you be Sir Nicklas 'Arbourne his own self! Which do seem right wonnerful and mirackless, sure-ly!"

"Oh hell! What's so wonderful about it, Bill?"

"That being a gen'leman—and so powerful rich, as they do tell, ee could work along o' we—so content and 'appy-'earted."

"Yes, I was content," sighed Nicholas, "and marvellously happy, at last. But now, and all in a moment, everything is changed and I—oh, damme, but here's a devilish nice mess, eh, Bill?"

"Ar, no question! A pretty kettle o' fish it be sure-ly, Sir Nicklas."

"Hush, none o' that! Mum, Bill, mum. Promise to keep it dark as long as possible, a secret between us. Is this understood?"

"Ar, sir, it be. And 'tis promise as I'll keep. So will I name ee Mist' Anthony still?"

"Of course."

"Well, Mist' Anthony sir, wot now?"

"Now, old fellow, since I'm dismissed, my only course is to—dismiss."

"Meaning as you'll tak' 'er at her word, sir, and go—leave us arl for good?"

"At once, Bill, and—for the good of all—I hope."

"Which can't nowise be, sir, not for Jarge, nor Joe no yet me, it can't."

"Thanks, Bill, I'm glad to know it."

"Ar, but Miss Priss'll miss ee right doleful and crool! How can us or any one comfort her without ee as be her very life. Think o' Miss Priss, sir!"

"I am, Bill. And while I do—ha—why didn't I use that whip, damn him."

"Eh, w'ip, sir? Oo and what——"

"Merely a yearning thought, old fellow."

"But, sir, oo's agoin' to comfort our li'l maid, I wonder?"

"I am, of course, Bill! Go with me as far as the road and I'll tell you how. . . ."

CHAPTER XXVI

Describes a "Splendorious" Tea-Party and the Comforting Wisdom of an Aunt

CONSEQUENTLY, a little later in this same eventful afternoon, as Priscilla fared demurely homeward from school, walking with leisured decorum "like Auntie Jo says all ladies should walk", she uttered a sudden, most unlady-like squeal of delighted surprise and, forgetting all other emotions, ran to meet the tall "gentlemanly" person so "elegantly attired", who was saluting her with hat gallantly aflourish.

"Ooh!" she gasped in an ecstasy. "How awful grand an' fine you look! Are you dressed in your very bestest things, my Anthony?"

"Some of them, sweetheart."

"Well, they're lovely, an' you look—splendorious!"

"And yet I miss the feel and clatter of my hob-nailed boots. But today, as you see, I'm adorned to take tea with a very lovely lady."

"Oh!" she sighed, her smile vanishing. "Please—who is she?"

"Well," he replied gravely, "some people hiss and call her Missss Prisss, but I, for my part, call her my sweetheart."

"Oh—do you—please do you mean—is she—me? And

you said it in poitry, too—but do you mean just me?"

"Of course, my precious, just and only you!"

"Oh, Anthony, am I your—lovely lady?"

"Yes, sweetheart, so long as you are Priscilla."

"And so I shall be—all my life long, though I haven't growed me very long yet—but you don't mind me not being any longer, do you?"

"No, because I shall always love you, however you are."

"Oh, Anthony . . . you do say the dearestannicest things! And now are you going to—take me out to tea with you?"

"That is the idea, my dear."

"And—will there be cake? Though I shan't mind if there isn't—but will there?"

"Cake?" he repeated, halting to ponder the question. "Ha, let's see now—yes, there will be plum cake, plain cake, seed cake, sponge cake, ham, bread and butter cut thin, watercress, lettuce and a bun or so——"

"Ooh!" exclaimed Priscilla, whispering above small hands clasped in an ecstasy. "Only you, my Anthony, could think of all the nice things I like most! Oh, you are so clever an' big an' wonderful as I don't know what I should do if I hadn't found you to be my Anthony that day you mended the old barn door. I think I should die without you!"

"No no, my dear, that is a very bad and evil thought, so think of those cakes instead."

"Yes, I am, plum an' seed an' sponge cakes—and buns —so let's hurry! Give me your hand."

Joined thus and very soon, they reached the Soaring

Lark, here to be welcomed by its smiling hostess, who curtsied, saying:

"Mr. Anson, I've done my best and d' hope as 'twill satisfy."

"Mrs. Lawler," he answered heartily, "your best always does and ever will!"

"Oh yes!" sighed Priscilla, beholding this well-laden table. "Oh, Mrs. Lawler, it's most wonderfully glorious, an' I thank you."

"Wherefore, I says 'bless you', Miss Priscilla. And, sir, the tea be noo-brewed and bell's at your elber."

Then down they sat together at this "truly festive" board which should have "groaned" but did not, probably because the many cakes were so light and the bread and butter cut so deliciously, not to say amazingly thin.

And now the lovely lady dispensed tea, with little finger daintily cocked and small hands rather tremulous by reason of the joy and wonder of it all; the cups abrim, she watched Anthony's first sip very anxiously and then enquired "as any grown-up lady should ought":

"I do hope your tea is like you like it?"

"Thank you, madam," he replied, bowing "p'litely like a gentleman should" and as she'd hoped he would; "indeed, my lady, I find it quite perfect!"

And so this memorable and happiest of meals progressed, until Priscilla, sighing but radiant-eyed, propounded the question:

"I wonder what Auntie Jo would say if she could see me now?"

At which precise moment Joanne, seated upon her tumbled bed, was saying:

"Dearest Aunt, what a comfort you are! I'm so very glad you agree I was right to get rid of him, though I don't think you should regard him as a—murderer."

"Why not, Joanne, if the brute intended murder, and we know he did, the letter tells us so! And, oh, think of your Charles and——"

"Aunt, do—not—call him 'my Charles', because he isn't and never can or could be——"

"Oh! But, my dear——"

"And don't 'Oh' at me. I can't bear it!"

"Very well, my dear—though I was afraid he was your choice—at one time."

"At what time, pray?"

"Before this serpent, Sir Nicholas, this slimy snake, came crawling to wriggle all about us, filling our too-credulous ears with his deceitful talk."

"I never saw him crawl or wriggle, Aunt, he couldn't —and snakes never talk! And whatever his sins, he was never cowardly or mean."

"However, my pet, we must be eternally grateful to your Char—I mean our Wolverton for warning and protecting us against this brutish villain and doing it all so nobly."

"Can you really think he did it nobly, Aunt?"

"Well, my dear, perhaps a better word would be 'art-fully'."

"Yes, and cunningly, cravenly, slyly, odiously, hate-fully, disgustingly and despicably!" said Joanne in one passionate breath.

"Could we but add the one word 'lyingly', my dear; and if only Anthony had been the splendid man we thought——"

"Did we, Aunt?"

"We did, Joanne! So tall, so gentle and strong——"

"Yes, brawny as a coalheaver!"

"So handsome and gay——"

"I never thought him handsome!"

"Oh, but he was——"

"No—Apollo Belvedere, Aunt!"

"True, Joanne, he was better looking, so much more character; in his face was power, my child, and with those grey eyes that seemed so clearly honest, with that gentle mouth that could smile so readily—and yet—oh dear me —if Wolverton tells the truth, this man who appeared so truly honest and honestly true is a—a fiend in human guise, a hypocritical snake in the grass—with blood on his horrible hands!"

"Snakes don't possess hands, Aunt, or——"

"No matter! If Wolverton is not lying, we know this —this two-legged monster for a horrid poisonous asp we have nourished in our devoted bosoms——"

"Good gracious, Aunt, we have done nothing so utterly loathsome!"

"Figuratively speaking, my child, we have most certainly, and considering his frightfully brutal nature, the wonder is we escaped with our lives, if we are to believe Wolverton——"

"Aunt, how preposterous——"

"But your Ch—Wolverton declares him a murderous ruffian and you have said he is brutal——"

"Yes, but—only now and then. And I suppose all men must be brutal when they fight."

"Then he is certainly a murderous fighter—to make

poor Charles all blood and black-eyes according to Doctor Stacey who——"

"He deserved it!"

"Joanne, what are you saying? Is it—can you mean——" And through white teeth clenched tightly she answered:

"Ch-Ch-Charles! His hateful letter!"

"Yes, my dear, it is a very hateful letter because hate inspired it! Ah, but for this, you would now be your own vital self, up and about, helping to save what is possible of that poor corn, instead of crouching here in misery like a distracted, mopish owl and 'Patience on a monument smiling—no—hissing at grief'—with your dear eyes so red and nice nose pink as a cherry!"

"Well, I don't care any more——"

"Because, thanks to Charles, you have driven joy away! And so," sighed Aunt Jemima in her gentle manner, "damn Charles!"

Joanne lifted drooping head to gaze at her ever-placid aunt in wide-eyed amazement; then:

"Oh!" she murmured, in awed tone. "You wise, wonderful, beloved comforter, will you say it again?"

"With pleasure! I damn Charles for your red eyes, rosy nose and spoiling such a perfect love affair——"

"Aunt—whatever—what love affair?"

"A more just and proper phrase would be 'love idyll', a truly Arcadian wooing. And I mean yours and Anthony's, of course."

"Oh, but—how can you imagine——"

"I don't! I know! Oh yes, I have been perfectly aware of it ever since you fell in love with him, and it has been growing upon you hourly until now you are hopelessly in love, indeed so terribly that it frightens you."

Joanne's sensitive lips quivered to deny; instead she turned and buried her face in the pillow.

"So, my dear, this is why I rejoice in our handyman's handiwork, meaning Charles's cuts and bangs and bruises and buffets! Also I add another swear, the word 'curse' for his hate-filled letter——"

"Oh," sighed Joanne, sitting up with despairing gesture, "but so hatefully—true!"

"A little, perhaps, my dear, a word or so here and there, but even were it all true you would still love your Anthony."

"But in spite of your wisdom and shrewdness, you once thought I could love—Charles, didn't you?"

"I had the uncomfortable idea that you might possibly marry him."

"How greatly mistaken you were! The mere idea of Charles for a husband nauseates and revolts me! Today the thought of marriage—with anyone, shocks and disgusts me so frightfully that I shall never marry now, Aunt, never!"

"Joanne, never is a long time!"

"Yes," said she, in voice suddenly very gentle, "so I've heard . . . sometimes it means a whole livelong day and sometimes—even a week. Oh, Aunt Jemima," she exclaimed, blinking to sudden, blinding tears, "this summer, this that I called my Glad Summer is the cruellest, the most . . . disappointing in . . . all my life!"

Then she was in those arms which all her life had been her never-failing comfort, and Aunt Jemima, smoothing this glorious hair that years ago had been termed "carrots", murmured consolingly:

"The summer is not ended yet, not quite, my dear one! And as for Anthony, I must now tell you something——"

"But, oh, Aunt, I must tell you he, Anthony—I mean Sir Nicholas—actually confessed to me and without the least shame that he had cheated and even lived by dishonest trickery."

"Did he tell you how and why, the whole story?"

"No, I wouldn't listen! I refused to hear any explanation. . . . I was too angry, too dreadfully shocked to hear any more."

"Then you shall hear now! For, Joanne, when I taxed him with loving you——"

"Oh—Aunt, did you? What did he say?"

"That he loved you more than life."

"Ah, why—why will he never say it to me?"

"Then, my dear, like the honourable gentleman he is, it was then he confessed to me his very eventful history, how and why he had been a cheating gambler, why he killed a man, with other quite dreadful incidents. And he told me all this, and I believe truthfully, that I might judge him worthy or no to wed you, if you could possibly love him. So, my dear, all he told me I will now recount to you that you in your turn may be his judge. . . ."

Plainly and very simply, Aunt Jemima told this tale, which done, she rose, saying:

"There, my dearest! I have told you all and nearly as possible in his own words. I will leave you now to think and judge for yourself between Anthony's tale and

Wolverton's letter. And remember, Joanne, summer is still with us."

"But it will soon be gone, Aunt, so pitiably soon!"

"Yes, my dear, as all worldly things must. But there is one blessing that remains to us through the passing years to be our joy and comfort in good times and evil, the one imperishable good that endures, I dare to believe, beyond even death—I mean the love that is truly sincere, because, Joanne, God is love."

CHAPTER XXVII

How Aunt Jemima Rose to the Occasion

EXUBERANT summer, chastened by the first wistful touch of gentle autumn, had dragged itself heavily six and three quarter days nearer grim winter, by Nicholas Anthony's precise reckoning, as Priscilla, clasping his ready hand, wended homeward through this radiant evening after yet another splendorious tea. They walked slowly and in an unusual silence, for Nicholas, being a truly sincere lover and therefore knowing himself quite unworthy, was losing all hope at last, while Priscilla's speechlessness may have been induced by cake; yet when at last she spoke it was to propound this rather startling question:

"Please, Anthony, do people's hearts go 'bang' when they break, or don't they? And if they do, does it hurt, or doesn't it?"

"Eh?" he exclaimed, halting and at a loss for words. "Well now—dash my wig! How . . . who . . . what do you know about such matters, my precious?"

"Not much. I only heard Anne tell Nancy in the dairy Auntie Jo's poor heart would break 'along of her being forsook so crool', and when I asked her if it would 'splode like guns do, all she said was, 'Lorks, Miss Priss, run away do'. So next time Auntie Jo went to cry at the pigsties I helped you to build so grand, I creeped after her, but she caught me, and when I told her I'd only come to hear if her poor heart would make a bang when it broke, she laughed at me, weeped at me and got fright-flee angry at me and said something that grieved me—doleful."

"What was that, sweetheart?"

"She told me to go away because I was a little horror. Everybody's always telling me to run away, but nobody ever called me such a awful thing before. So now, my Anthony, will you tell me if hearts——"

"No, my little Angel of Hope, you shall tell me about far better and lovelier things. Let's sit here under the hedge—now, let me hear about your Auntie Jo. She weeps, does she, sweetheart?"

"Yes, and when I catch her at it she says it's a cold and blows her nose."

"Bless her!" he murmured.

"Oh, why—for blowing her nose?"

"For weeping, my dear one. You see, tears make beauty more tenderly beautiful——"

"Oh no, Anthony! They only make Auntie Jo's nose pink and her eyes red, like when I caught her hiding her sobs in the pigsties——"

"Was she, by George!"

"No, by herself. George was in the barn with Bill when he told me to tell you as how things was getting that doleful, another pair of hands was needed with arms around one for the good of all, and he said as you'd know. So if you do, will you tell me all. . . . Oh my—there's Aunt 'Mima coming to meet us; no, she's waiting by the pigsties to send me to bed! She looks fright-flee stern and gotobedatoncey, doesn't she, Anthony?"

o

"Yes, sweetheart, I'm afraid she does! I wonder why."

"Oh, I s'pose she thinks you've kept me a bit late. But never mind, I'll say it was my fault——"

"My dear little champion!" said he and, pausing, stooped and kissed her, after which they approached Aunt Jemima where she stood an almost forbidding, very stately figure in bonnet and Paisley shawl. Nevertheless, and forthwith, Priscilla broke into instant speech:

"Aunt Mima, please—if you're going to blame my Anthony for being late, please don't, 'cause it were all my own fault, there was so much to eat and talk about. So now I s'pose you've come to say I must getreadyfor-bedthismomentmiss and so I will, like a most 'bedient person what I am—though my Lady Moon is just begin-ning to peep an' smile at me. But I'll go drackly-minute when you say I must."

But in voice unexpectedly gentle, Aunt Jemima replied:

"On the contrary, my dear, tonight you are staying up to have supper with us——"

"Ooh!" cried Priscilla, dancing in an ecstasy of blissful surprise. "Thank you. Oh, thank you lotsanlots! Oh, how very splen-dorious!"

"Yes, my dear, I mean it to be!" said Aunt Jemima, almost grimly. "When your Lady Moon rises tonight I hope she will smile down on such happiness as shall make this the gladdest summer that ever was. So, Pris-cilla, go and put on your prettiest dress, wash and do your hair, of course, and should your Auntie Joanne ask why, tell her I suggest she does the same because this is an occasion that can never happen again. Tell Anne to hang the champagne in the well to cool it and set the port not too near the fire and that the goose must have a slow oven. Can you remember all that, my dear?"

"Yes, Aunt, yes—me! Supper! My prettiest frock and —oh, you 'dorable Aunt!" And housewards sped Priscilla on dancing feet

"And now," said Nicholas, venturing speech at last, "pray have you no word for your dutiful nephew and once humbly devoted handyman?"

"Yes, Sir Nicholas, several!"

"Now Lord love me!" he exclaimed. "Aunt, my dear, why so coldly aloof? Have I done anything to offend you?"

"Yes, nothing!" she retorted. "You have done, are doing and always will do nothing, it seems! This is why I am here."

"Aunt, if you mean——"

"Considering you were such a very able handyman, so quick and adroit, such a supremely deft card-sharper, you are the clumsiest, dullest, most awkward lover that could ever possibly be."

"Yes," he said humbly, "yes, I am indeed. But there are many reasons why——"

"Name one!"

"Love!" he answered. "Yes, and the real thing at last! It's got me—body and soul! She so purely sweet and I—so unworthy that—oh, damme, I shall never dare approach her—until she calls or gives me some sign."

"Which she probably never will, my poor, sentimentally craven, do-nothing nephew, because she is as ridiculously proud as you are absurdly humble."

"Then, oh, Aunt Jemima, what are we to do about it? What do you suggest?"

"You have been in love before, of course?"

"Yes, at least I thought so at the time, but never with anyone comparable with Joanne, and, ah, my dear, never so truly, never so—reverently as now. Reverently—this makes all the difference, Aunt; this is why I feel so helpless and ask your advice."

"Not mine, Sir Nicholas; your own past experience should guide you and——"

"Not with Joanne, Aunt! Ah—never!"

"She, like the others, Nephew, is merely a woman!"

"No! She is *the* woman, Aunt! The one, yes, by God, the only one in all this world for me. Oh, Aunt Jemima, can't you understand?"

"Nicholas-Anthony, I do!" said she in her usual gentle manner, slipping her hand within his ready arm. "Please to walk me as far as the lane and back. Yes," she continued as they strolled thitherward, "I understand so well that here am I upon your arm, my dear, resolved to end all this proudly woeful and highly sentimental nonsense. So now, Anthony, answer me this, and think well. Loving Joanne as I'm quite sure you do, with all that is best in your nature, have you ever told her so, actually?"

"Of course, my dear! Besides, she knows I adore her."

"Oh yes, she knows and has done for weeks, but have you told her in as many words?"

"Yes, I . . . I think so. I must have done."

"Well then, what was her answer?"

"Aunt," said he, coming to sudden halt, "I—don't know! She must have said something, but just what I —can't remember. Which is confoundedly odd——"

"Oh no, which proves you never uttered those words, my very blundering, extremely clumsy handyman!"

"No, I can't have done. But, since she knows, what difference can it make?"

"Every difference, Mr. Dunderhead! Yes, all the difference in the world! A woman may know a man loves her, but she needs to hear him tell her so and as often as possible."

"Then, by heavens, Aunt, she shall hear me, yes and at once, so pray let's go!"

"Where, Nephew?"

"To the house or wherever she is. Oh, my dear wise Aunt, take me to her."

"My dear Anthony, I should be perfect fool of an aunt if I did! Joanne must not see us together or guess we have talked, or her pride will be up in arms, instead of she in yours——"

"In my arms!" he repeated, turning to glance at the distant house where lights were beginning to twinkle. "In my arms! To have and to hold——"

"For better or worse, my dear! And, of course, there will be 'worse', now and then. Remember her fiery hair —and at school they called her 'carrots' and 'snapper' and 'spitfire'! Are you warned, Nephew?"

"So much so that I long for sight of our beloved snapping spitfire; when and where may I see her?"

"Hereabouts and probably when the Lady Moon peeps at you over the tree-tops yonder. Just so soon as I can induce her, all unknowing, to walk into the arms of the one man in all creation who can be her happiness. And I send her to you, Anthony-Nicholas, because her happiness is very dear to me and—her choice mine also."

"Oh, Aunt!" he murmured. "Aunt Jemima, you honour me above all men."

"Yes, Anthony, I do indeed!"

"Dearest of aunts, you make me so very proud, and yet—so humble that I don't know what to say——"

"Don't try, my dear. Say it all to Joanne. So now, Master Impatient Lover, while you watch the moon, I'll go and inform my wilful, woeful niece how the dew is so heavy tonight that no one can possibly walk in it without wet feet and an ensuing, sniffling cold—whereupon she will instantly discover that a walk is the one blessing left to her in a dismal universe, and may possibly quote that old song: 'Oh it's dabbling in the dew that makes the milkmaids fair', and out she will come to dabble! So be prepared, Anthony, and God bless you both!"

"And you also!" he rejoined fervently. "And now," said he, more lightly, "by her gracious leave, Nicholas is going to kiss Anthony's aunt in token of their united love and gratitude. . . ."

This done, Aunt Jemima laughed happily, straightened her bonnet and said:

"Remember the goose, my dear!"

"Goose?" he repeated vaguely.

"Goose, Nephew. In the oven, Anthony. For supper, Nicholas! So pray keep within sound of the bell."

CHAPTER XXVIII

Which, Though the last Chapter, is not Quite so Sentimental as Might be Expected

NEVER, thought Nicholas, no, never in all his born days had the moon taken such an infernal time to rise—she crawled, she crept like a confounded slug or snail, while here stood he, leaning against the pigsty wall, listening, watching, hoping—and all in vain so far! Oh well, if the damn moon never rose and Joanne consequently did not venture out—then to the house he'd go, snatch her up and bear her out into this fragrant, late-summer night, by main force; and if she ventured to rebel—one struggle or a single futile kick, he would kiss her to helpless submission! And then, by Saint George and his beastly dragon, he would tell her plainly what a beloved fool she had been to waste so much precious time—very nearly seven miserable days! Though, to be sure, she was vastly too good for such hard-bitten roustabout as he was, or had been. However, if she did actually or could possibly love him (and, ha, the wonder of it!) he would insist upon marrying her instantly . . . and then . . . a home at last! A home made and blest by her presence! A home, no matter where, though certainly not Grayladies, that resplendent rabbit warren; no, a house much smaller and more dearly intimate. . . . And if, later on, they were blest with a child . . . children . . . they would move into houses ever larger and more commodious. . . . A family. This thought so enthralled him that he forgot all else, until he blinked to a sudden radiance—and there was the moon at last, peeping down at him above motionless treetops. Yes, there indeed was Her Serene Majesty, this pale most lovely Lady of the Night, glorifying all things with her gentle magic, an all-pervading beatitude, and: Never, thought Nicholas, never in all his roving on sea or land had Her Moonship been quite so beautiful as now, on this night of nights—this good, fair English moon that would, he hoped, show the good, fair English maid who was coming to fill his eager arms, if only for a moment, of this he was certain, but who might, perhaps, bless and make his life complete as only she could, if only she would—this he could but hope. Yet even now, mindful of their last meeting, her fierce anger and bitter scorn, Hope languished, Doubt assailed him, and Despair, this merciless giant, smote him. . . . Ah, but then upon the night's solemn, all-pervading hush there broke a very earthly sound, not loud, but so extremely human that tormenting Doubt fled instantly, Giant Despair, forgetting to be grim, lumbered away down to the nether regions, while Nicholas, starting and startled, turned and beheld Joanne in the act of sneezing again: she as suddenly espying him, in this most unromantic moment, sneezed, turned to fly and found herself in his arms . . . and in this so yearned-for moment of moments all he said was:

"Good great heavens—you're catching cold!" And, yielding to these very comfortably possessive arms, what she replied was:

"So much the better! And if I sink into a rapid decline and perish, so much the better still!"

"Which," said he, folding her closer, "would be damn preposterously absurd. What you have to do for both our sakes is to live, Joanne, and go on living to make old bones, because——"

"What a—horribly hideous suggestion!" she exclaimed, moving slightly in these arms—almost as if she nestled.

"Because——" he repeated, then paused, took a deep breath, but before he could utter the word as yet unspoken, she demanded:

"Because what, pray?" And remembering her own tantalising answer, he replied:

"Just because, Joanne!" Then while she strove, as expected, to break from these prisoning arms, he voiced that most necessary word, at last uttered it repeatedly, as thus:

"Because I love you, Joanne. I always have loved you. I always shall love you. I loved you with our first glance. I shall love you with our last. I love you so much more than life that life is worthless without you, because you are your strong, brave, glorious self and I am—only me, this poor, adoring Anthony who is trying to tell you— how I love you."

Round his neck came her soft arms, back went her stately head to show him, and the Lady Moon, the beauty of a face made lovely by ineffable tenderness . . . the glitter of tears that made her eyes only the more beautiful, or so thought Nicholas, and (wise at last) told her so, then, having kissed away these happy tears, would have freed her, but:

"Oh, my Anthony, my handyman," she murmured. "Stoop your dear head!" And so, for the first time, she kissed him. Then she was up in his arms, lying upon his breast, and the moon now so very bright above them that Joanne sighed:

"What a glorious night, Anthony; but supposing we are seen—like this?"

"What matter? Though we can't be, we shan't be—however——!" So saying he bore her into the nearest pigsty and there sat down, with Joanne upon his knees. "Now," said he, tilting her head back that he might see her eyes, "the idea is to get a certain fact into this beautiful dear lovely foolish head of yours that is really mine or soon will be, the fact that Nicholas Anthony Harbourne is asking, no, is sueing, wooing, pleading, praying and imploring——"

"And all this, my dearest, in a pigsty!"

"Yes, Joanne, for there never were such pigsties as these because I built love into them with every brick and, besides, you hallowed them with your precious tears——"

"And pray, how do you know I—ah, Priscilla! Of course! The little wretch came——"

"Not so; a small, bright angel appeared——"

"Came stealing here so very slyly, hoping my heart would break——"

"Wondering, in her sweet innocence, if your 'poor heart would 'splode like guns do'. How is your heart at present?"

"Quite well, thank you!"

"Let me hear. Lie still!"

"Oh—Anthony——!"

"Ah, Joanne! The poor, dear thing is thumping like a trip hammer!"

"And no wonder—when I'm lying helpless in the grasp of——"

"Your own humble, adoring Anthony. Yes, you are in your right place at last——"

"In a pigsty, my Anthony!"

"Sacred to me, Joanne, for this glorious hour and because here and now, with you in my embrace, I love you so truly that I hardly dare touch or kiss you; this is the odd, sentimental sort of fellow I am——"

"And, oh," she murmured, nestling closer, "this is exactly the odd sort of fellow I hoped and dreamed might find me some day—who, scarcely daring to touch, clasped and held me so close, and, being afraid to kiss—kissed me until I——"

Nicholas did.

High rose the Moon's Serene Majesty, and higher, to beam down upon these happy ones who thus seated in a pigsty, where pig as yet had never grunted, would not have exchanged it for any palace on earth because here with them and of them was such love as hallowed both it and themselves. And thus in a content ineffable they might have remained, but . . .

"Oh!" sighed Joanne at last. "There is the bell calling us to supper!"

"A goose!" moaned Anthony.

"And prepared especially by Aunt Jemima herself!"

"And myself too happy to eat!" sighed Anthony. And he verily believed this until, as they stepped from moonlight into lamp and candle-glow, there stole a mouth-watering fragrance, waking a hunger that clamoured. . . .

There have been other geese possibly as well-cooked and seasoned, it is just possible, but not so for Nicholas; indeed this particular goose was to remain for him an abiding and fragrant memory. And when at last this truly unforgettable bird had made a right noble end, Aunt Jemima leaned back in her high-backed chair to enquire:

"My dears, have you decided when and where you propose to set up housekeeping?"

"In some such cosy old farmstead as this," said Nicholas decisively.

"At Grayladies!" replied Joanne, gentle of voice and look, though more decisively.

"But, Joanne dear, I discharged those hordes of servants —at least I believe I did."

"Then, Anthony dearest, we will engage others."

"Aha!" he exclaimed, meeting the witchery of her eyes. "Oh? Very well, for I believe you can make even that confounding magnificence a home by the mere spell of your presence."

"And when is your wedding, my dears?"

"Next week!" said Anthony.

"In about five or six months!" said Joanne.

"Very well," laughed Aunt Jemima, "it shall be in a month. And so, Joanne, in spite of storm, stress, malice, tears, pride, sentimentality and other nonsense, this has proved a glad year of summer, as I foretold!"

"Yes, you dear and wonderful aunt!" sighed Joanne.

"The first of many such, I hope and believe!" said Anthony.

"But, ah, my dears, as the Past fades behind us to be mostly forgotten, the Future looms before us, soon to be a most vital reality. So now, pray, Anthony, refill the glasses and we will drink to the Future—that God in his mercy may bless it to us and you to one another. May age never dim the light in your eyes, and the years serve only to knit you closer in a union blest and made sacred by that love which, being of God, is a joy unfailing, with a strength to endure all things. And so . . . Oh, my dears, God bless you to each other."

Scarcely had they drunk this toast and very reverently than Priscilla, sleepy of look and drowsy of voice, enquired rather plaintively:

"Please can I be drank to—and blessed, too."

"Oh, my poor, dear child, you are actually drooping with sleep——"

"Oh no, with goose, Aunt. I'm not very sleepy—only a teeny bit, so can't I be drank to and blest?"

"Yes, my precious, you shall!" said Nicholas, and rising, glass in hand: "Aunt Jemima, Joanne, dearest of ladies," said he, "the toast is your beloved and my ever dear sweetheart, Mistress Priscilla. May she grow in beauty as in grace to love and be right well loved by all, yet by none more truly than her own Anthony. Ladies, Mistress Priscilla!"

"And now," said Aunt Jemima, setting down her glass, "sweet Mistress Priscilla, I bid your ladyship to bed and sweet dreams. Come and kiss good night."

"Oh, Aunt 'Mima, how splen-dorious you are and everything so lovely tonight! So, my Anthony, will you please ride me up to bed on your shoulder?"

"Of course, sweetheart; ask your Auntie Jo to lead the way."

So up the broad, old stair they went all three, waking the echoes of this aged homestead with their happy voices, while Aunt Jemima, gazing down at the massive logs that smouldered as usual on that wide and generous hearth, thought of the children yet to be, the unborn generations, and breathed a sigh that was a prayer of gratitude for life and love and the peaceful security of this small though mighty and most blessed isle that was —her England.

Now here this truly sentimental tale should end, and so it would but for three of its characters; and firstly, Aunt Jemima, who says, in her gentle, placid manner:

"My dear Mr. Jeffery, we are all very grateful to you for bringing us to life and making us known to so very many people who will read us, I hope, for your sake, and will like us enough to make us their friends for our own sakes, but, my dear, couldn't you contrive a more comprehensive end to our novel?"

And, secondly, little Priscilla, who enquired:

"Oh, please won't you write some more of me, especially how I bridesmaided my Auntie Jo when our vicar turned my Anthony into my one and onliest uncle?"

And, thirdly, Bill, chief of the sturdy, hard-working Faithful Three, who suggests and rather shyly:

"Mist' Farnol, sir, don't ee think as 'ow you ought for to tell summat o' the folkses' wunnerful surprise, ar and re-j'icing to find as how Mistus Joanne's handyman were their very own landlord and right praper un as 'e be, sure-ly and no question—don't ee, sir?"

"But," says I, "should I do so, our warm, glad summer would pass into chill winter, Harbourne's smiling fields and lush meadows become a windswept desolation where no birds sing, a solitude veiled in mist bleak from the distant sea."

Therefore, while the sun beams, birds carol and trees rustle leaves already touched by the brush of that lovely artist, Autumn, I deem it best to leave these characters, these children pen-begot, in the secure happiness and peaceful content of mid-Victorian England, that home of ancient freedom, piety and of plenty. Which seems to us of this war-worn, harassed generation no more than merest dream, yet a dream which I pray shall be made real, stronger and more vital than ever before, when we as a nation shall prove ourselves, once again, fit and worthy.

Jeffery Farnol.